# The Ratbridge Chronicles

Mildevish Charts & Maps

# WORSE THINGS HAPPEN AT SEA!

## A TALE OF
### PIRATES, POISON, AND MONSTERS

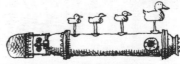
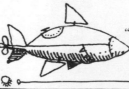

# WORSE THINGS HAPPEN AT SEA!

### A TALE OF
### PIRATES, POISON, AND MONSTERS

by Alan Snow

**OXFORD**

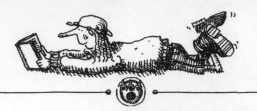

# OXFORD
## UNIVERSITY PRESS

Great Clarendon Street, Oxford OX2 6DP

Oxford University Press is a department of the University of Oxford.
It furthers the University's objective of excellence in research, scholarship,
and education by publishing worldwide in

Oxford   New York

Auckland   Cape Town   Dar es Salaam   Hong Kong   Karachi
Kuala Lumpur   Madrid   Melbourne   Mexico City   Nairobi
New Delhi   Shanghai   Taipei   Toronto

With offices in

Argentina   Austria   Brazil   Chile   Czech Republic   France   Greece
Guatemala   Hungary   Italy   Japan   Poland   Portugal   Singapore
South Korea   Switzerland   Thailand   Turkey   Ukraine   Vietnam

Oxford is a registered trade mark of Oxford University Press
in the UK and in certain other countries

Text and illustrations © Alan Snow 2010

The moral rights of the author have been asserted

Database right Oxford University Press (maker)

First published 2010

British Library Cataloguing in Publication Data

Data available

ISBN: 978-0-19-271965-2

1 3 5 7 9 10 8 6 4 2

Printed in Great Britain

To Issy, whose father is not very good at drawing horses
& Theo, Maya, Finn, Tom and Ruby

# WORSE THINGS HAPPEN AT SEA!

### A TALE OF
### PIRATES, POISON, AND MONSTERS

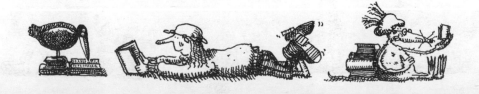

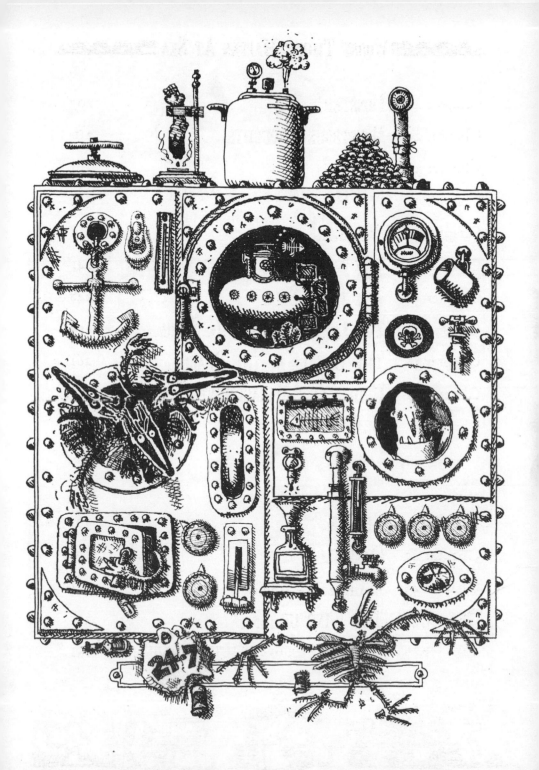

# Johnson's Taxonomy
## of Trolls and Creatures

### Cabbage Island
A legendary island that is supposed to be in the southern Pacific. Said to be the home of strange plants with incredible powers. While it is not known if this island exists it is mentioned in many travelogues of the region and turns up in folklore surrounding cheese and health.

### Crow
The crow is an intelligent bird, capable of living in many environments. Usually they are charming company, but should be kept from providing the entertainment. Failure to do so may result in tedium, for while intelligent, crows seem to lack taste in the choice of music, and conversational topics.

### Albatross
A true sea bird that has been known to spend up to 10 years without ever visiting land. Has large wingspan (3.5 metres). Can live up to 85 years and pairs for life.

### Boxtrolls
A sub-species of the common troll, they are very shy, so live inside a box. These they gather from the backs of large shops. They are somewhat troublesome creatures—as they have a passion for everything mechanical and no understanding of the concept of ownership (they steal anything which is not bolted down and, more often than not, anything which is). It is very dangerous to leave tools lying about where they might find them.

### Cheese
Wild English Cheeses live in bogs. This is unlike their French cousins who live in caves. They are nervous beasties, that eat grass by night, in the meadows and woodlands. They are also of very low intelligence, and are panicked by almost anything that catches them unawares. Cheese make easy quarry for hunters, being rather easier to catch than a dead sheep.

### Guillemot (paid entry)
Famously the name of the founder of the fabulous south sea trading company and mail order business. Providers of exotic and budget items for every home. Send a stamped addressed envelope and you will be amazed at just how quickly we respond (3 year delivery guaranteed).

## The Members

Members of the secretive Ratbridge Cheese Guild, that was thought to have died out after the 'Great Cheese Crash'. It was an evil organization that rigged the cheese market, and doctored and adulterated lactose-based food stuffs.

## Grandfather (William)

Arthur's guardian and carer. Grandfather lived underground for many years in a cave home where he pursued his interests in engineering. But after some rather unusual events both Arthur and his grandfather found themselves with a new home in the former petshop now rented by Willbury Nibble and shared with boxtrolls and Titus the cabbagehead. He now wakes up late, then spends his days in the company of Willbury and all their new friends, and has been known to sneak off on his own to the Nag's Head tavern for a crafty pint and bag of pork scratchings with a pickled egg. Now relieved of the sole care of Arthur, his favourite pastime is reading in bed with his own bucket of cocoa.

## Rats

Rats are known to be some of the most intelligent of all rodents, and to be considerably more intelligent than many humans. They are known to have a passion for travel, and be extremely adaptable. They often live in a symbiotic relationship with humans.

## Legendary Monsters

Often found wandering the southern sea and should be avoided at all cost, unless you are the owner of a Guillemot Monster-repelling Kit. These are available by mail order (see entry for Guillemot). These monsters are known to reside on many islands and thought to be the last remaining dinosaurs on the planet. Last confirmed sighting—Tokyo 1723.

## Shopping Birds

A once common bird that has now become rare due to its blatant consumerism and lack of intelligence.

## Trotting Badgers

Trotting badgers are some of the nastiest creatures to be found anywhere. With their foul temper, rapid speed, and razor-sharp teeth, it cannot be stressed just how unpleasant and dangerous these creatures are. It is only their disgusting stench that gives warning of their proximity, and when smelt it is often too late.

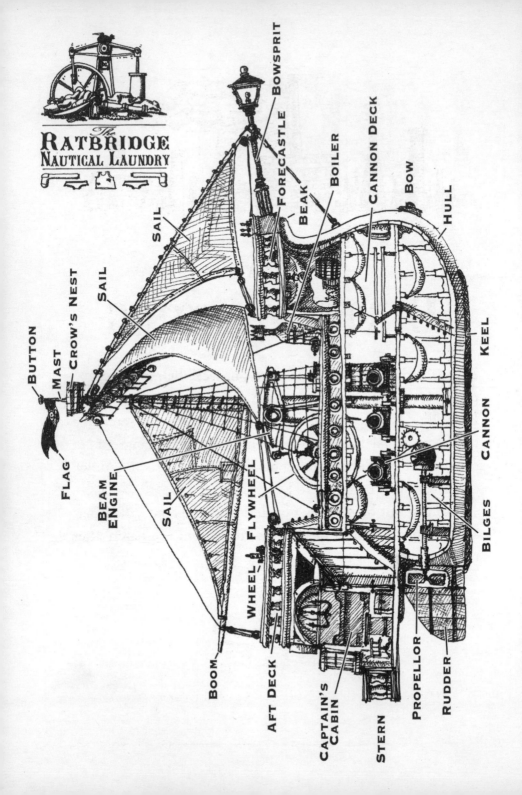

The RATBRIDGE NAUTICAL LAUNDRY

BUTTON

MAST

CROW'S NEST

SAIL

SAIL

SAIL

FORECASTLE BOWSPRIT

BEAK

BOILER

CANNON DECK

BOW

HULL

KEEL

FLAG

BEAM ENGINE

SAIL

WHEEL FLYWHEEL

AFT DECK

CAPTAIN'S CABIN

STERN

PROPELLOR

RUDDER

BILGES

CANNON

BOOM

*The Ratbridge Nautical Laundry*

## Chapter 1

# DIRTY WASHING

Arthur and his grandfather were on deck, helping pack up piles of washing to be returned to the customers of the Ratbridge Nautical Laundry. Around them the rats and pirates were all hard at work checking lists, hanging out clothes to dry, and emptying baskets of dirty washing down the hatch into the bilges to be washed.

'Almost out of washing powder!' shouted a rat called Bert as he tipped a shovel of pink powder down the hatch after the washing.

*He tipped a shovel of pink powder down the hatch after the washing*

'You don't half get through a lot,' commented Arthur.

'Not surprising given the state of this place's underwear. Takes some shifting,' smiled Grandfather.

Then there was a commotion on the towpath. They turned to see policemen and an angry mob heading in their direction.

'What now?' muttered Tom, the worried-looking captain and laundry manager.

The police reached the gangplank and the unruly mob stopped behind them.

'String them up!'

'Hanging's too good for them!'

'Shame! Shame!'

Tom led the crew to the top of the gangplank to face the crowd.

One of the policemen came forward, pulled a piece of paper from his jacket, looked up at Tom and spoke.

*Policemen and an angry mob*

'Sir, are you in charge of this operation?'

' ... Yes ... '

'Well, I hereby arrest you and your crew.'

'SHAME ON THEM!' cried the mob.

'What have we done?' Tom and the crew had kept the town's laundry and their noses clean ever since they had opened.

'Earlier this morning the famous Countess Grogforth visited the town on a ceremonial shopping trip and was shocked to see the town's underwear flying from your rigging in a rude display.'

'We're a laundry! It's just drying clothes,' Tom protested.

Kipper, the pirate by his side, was going red with indignation. 'Yes. And it's the town's clothes!'

'That is not my concern. Countess Grogforth passed comment on the unfashionable and coarse nature of the said underwear, and was so shocked that she fainted away, damaging her wig, her high born sensibilities, and the town's pride. She is now seeking compensation for that injury and the town is suing for damages to its reputation.'

*The damaged wig*

'This is ridiculous!' whispered Arthur.

His friends remained silent.

'As a law officer of this town I hereby serve you all with this arrest warrant and summons to appear at court at ten tomorrow morning. You're to remain here on the ship under police guard until we accompany you to court,' the policeman said. Then, pointing to the washing in the rigging with his truncheon, he added: 'And take that washing in or there'll be further charges.'

Leaning in towards the crew so that he couldn't be heard by the mob around him, he quietly added, 'Did you get the stains out of my vest?'

*The stained vest*

*The police set up camp*

## Chapter 2

# No Way Out?

The police set up camp at the bottom of the gangplank, and ordered the mob to disperse.

'On your way!'

The mob went quiet and looked a little uneasy. Then a rather runkled man came forward.

'Can we collect our washing first?'

Looking at how dirty the mob seemed, the officer nodded and a queue formed on the gangplank.

'Give them their washing.'

The crew did as they were told but this just added to their sense of injustice. As the last of the mob disappeared down the towpath Kipper shook his head.

'After all the trouble we take with their smalls . . . '

'Next time we should starch all their underwear.'

'There might not be a next time,' Tom said with resignation.

*'Next time we should starch all their underwear.'*

'What are you going to do?' asked Arthur. 'This is all totally unfair.'

'The first thing is to get hold of Willbury. He's a lawyer and will know what to do,' Grandfather replied.

'But we're not allowed off the ship,' said Tom, eyeing the policemen.

'We could attack the Squeakers, and throw them in the canal,' offered Bert.

'No, that would only cause more trouble. It would be better for someone to sneak off the ship, and go and tell Willbury what's happened.'

*'We could attack the Squeakers and throw them in the canal.'*

'But how?' asked Arthur.

Marjorie, their friend and chief laundry engineer, spoke. 'Wait until darkness and use the submarine?'

There was a raising of eyebrows. Although the submarine had been attached to the side of the ship ever since the crew could remember, it hadn't been used in years, and no one was really sure if it was still in working order. Marjorie, however, was not one to be put off by such concerns.

'I'll have a look at it and see if it needs any attention. It's moored on the other side of the ship, out of sight, and if we can get it going we can submerge, go along the canal to a place where the police can't see us, resurface, and then go and tell Willbury what's happened.'

'Sounds like a plan,' smiled Kipper, the largest of the pirates. 'Who is going to go?'

'Well I think I will have to,' said Marjorie, 'as I do know how to make the thing work, but I will need some help.'

Tom looked at Arthur and Grandfather. 'I think it would be best if we got you both off the ship. There is no need for you to end up in court.'

Arthur had mixed feelings about this. He agreed that it would be good to get his grandfather off the ship, and he had always wanted to have a go in the submarine, but leaving his friends to face the charges seemed a little disloyal.

Marjorie was watching him and spoke. 'This is a dangerous mission and I need you to help me drive the submarine.'

Arthur nodded and felt better.

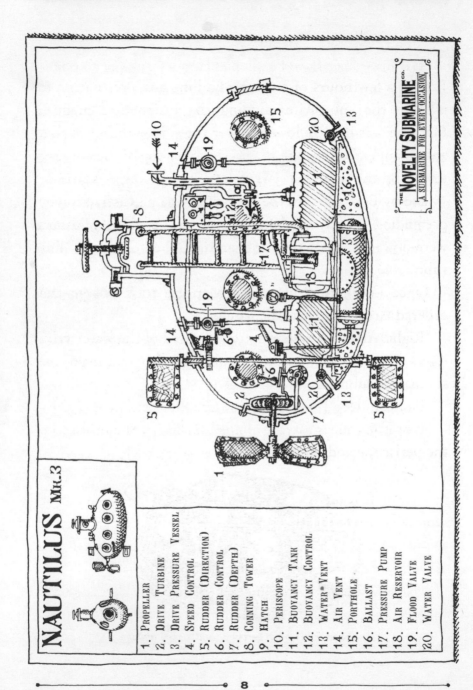

NAUTILUS Mᴋ.3

THE NOVELTY SUBMARINE Co.
A SUBMARINE FOR EVERY OCCASION

1. PROPELLER
2. DRIVE TURBINE
3. DRIVE PRESSURE VESSEL
4. SPEED CONTROL
5. RUDDER (DIRECTION)
6. RUDDER CONTROL
7. RUDDER (DEPTH)
8. CONNING TOWER
9. HATCH
10. PERISCOPE
11. BUOYANCY TANK
12. BUOYANCY CONTROL
13. WATER VENT
14. AIR VENT
15. PORTHOLE
16. BALLAST
17. PRESSURE PUMP
18. AIR RESERVOIR
19. FLOOD VALVE
20. WATER VALVE

\* \* \*

It took a few hours of secretive fiddling and preparation to prepare the sub. After finding the instruction manual, Marjorie was quietly lowered over the side with her toolkit and disappeared through the hatch on the top of the conning tower. By the time that darkness fell everything was ready.

Led by Bert, most of the crew then set up a distraction by pretending to play cards, while the group of submariners were lowered over the side and climbed into the tiny submarine.

Once inside the submarine Marjorie took charge and ordered Arthur to close the hatch.

'Right. Arthur, I want you to take hold of the water valve levers. They allow water into tanks and that will make the submarine submerge.'

'Not too deep I hope,' replied Grandfather.

'Not if Arthur is careful,' smiled Marjorie. She pushed up the periscope and looked about.

*She pushed up the periscope and looked about*

'OK. Motor started, and Arthur . . . open the valves.'

Arthur swung both of the levers and there was a gurgling from the pipes. They were on their way!

*Arthur swung both of the levers*

Up above the water, only the ducks noticed as a strange bent pipe started moving away from the back of the ship and heading off down the canal.

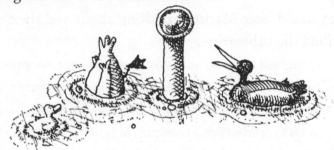

*Only the ducks noticed*

'I think we'll have to go quite a way under water or we'll be seen when we come up,' said Marjorie as she scanned the canal through the periscope.

The submarine moved slowly down the canal until they were well out of sight, but before Marjorie could give the order to surface there was a very loud CLANG! and the submarine stopped suddenly with an enormous jolt.

Inside the sub there were cries and yelps as the crew fell to the floor and the lights went out.

'What was that?' came Marjorie's voice.

'Is everybody all right?' asked Arthur.

'I think so. My whiskers are a bit bent but otherwise I'm all right,' Tom replied.

'Grandfather?'

There was no reply, and Arthur felt suddenly very worried.

'Grandfather? Are you all right?' There was still no reply.

'Marjorie, get the lights back on! There is something very wrong.'

They could hear Marjorie fiddling about and then a dim light filled the submarine.

Arthur turned to look at Grandfather where he lay on the floor. The old man had his eyes closed and was very still.

Arthur rushed to him and lifted his head from the floor. As he did so Grandfather started to stir.

'What's happened?' he muttered.

'We have to get him out of here. Can we surface?'

Marjorie was looking concerned.

'I hope so. We're far enough away not to be spotted by the policemen, but I don't know what's happened. Arthur, you close the valves and I'll fill the tanks with air to get us up.'

As the tanks were filled there was hissing, and a groaning from both Grandfather and the submarine.

Marjorie looked up the periscope. 'We're not rising. We

must be caught on something. Tom, have a look out of the porthole at the front.'

The rat peered out into the gloom of the canal water.

*The rat peered out into the gloom*

'It looks like a bedstead. It's caught around our bow.'

'Let's put as much air into the tanks as we can. That should do it.'

She moved a lever and there was more hissing and bubbling.

'What's happening with the bedstead?'

Tom looked out again. 'Seems to be holding us down.'

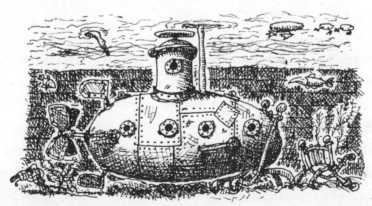

*'It looks like a bedstead.'*

Marjorie gave another push on the lever and the submarine finally broke free. It shot upwards, broke the surface and rose like a breaching whale, before finally splashing down and settling.

*It shot upwards, broke the surface, and rose like a breaching whale*

Again the crew found themselves shaken to the floor, but as Arthur was cradling Grandfather's head he managed to guard him from further injury—though the old man still let out a pitiful moan.

After taking a few moments to recover Marjorie climbed up the conning tower and opened the hatch.

'Let's get Grandfather back to the shop and find Willbury.'

It took a lot of effort and a great deal of care to get Grandfather out of the submarine and back to the shop, and by the time they had Grandfather tucked up in bed, Arthur, Kipper, Tom, and Marjorie were even more bruised and exhausted.

Willbury listened with horror to the happenings of the day as he tended to Grandfather.

'I will try to get time to prepare for the case once I have settled the patient.'

Tom and Kipper thanked him and then set off back to the ship with Marjorie, not really looking forward to the return journey in the submarine.

*It took a lot of effort and a great deal of care to get*
*Grandfather out of the submarine*

*Stuffed into the dock was the entire crew*

Chapter 3

# THE SCALES OF JUSTICE

As the last toll of the Town Hall bell faded at ten o'clock the next morning, the clerk of the court spoke. 'All rise!'

The court rose and all went quiet as in shuffled the decrepit form of Judge Podger. Stuffed into the dock was the entire crew of the Ratbridge Nautical Laundry and standing on the floor of the court were Willbury Nibble QC and Mr Smarmy Slingshot the prosecutor. Willbury was looking flushed, tired, and very glum after a bad night trying to tend Grandfather and preparing for the case.

He whispered to Marjorie, who was by his side.

'They're in for it. Podger will have them hanged if he gets a chance. I've had to try to deal with him before.'

As soon as the judge was seated the clerk of the court spoke again.

'The court may be seated. First case. Countess Grogforth and the Town versus The Ratbridge Nautical Laundry.'

'Very well,' Judge Podger said as he eyed the dock. 'Ten years each. Send them down!'

*'Ten years each. Send them down!'*

'SIR! I am acting on behalf of the Ratbridge Nautical Laundry and they plead not guilty,' Willbury protested.

'Damn you, man. I have a tea appointment at eleven.'

Mr Smarmy Slingshot now spoke.

'Sir, I would also like the case to be heard by your graciousness as both the Countess and the Town are seeking compensation for the criminal action of the members of the laundry.'

'Very well. But keep it short.'

'May I call the first witness, sir?'

'Get on with it!'

'Call the Countess Grogforth.'

The doors at the back of the courtroom opened and in walked two policemen supporting what looked like an Egyptian mummy. The policemen guided the mummy to the stand, where it curtsied to the judge and sat.

Mr Smarmy Slingshot began his questioning.

'Madam, can you tell me what has happened to you?'

The mummy made some muffled moaning noises and then went quiet.

*The policemen guided the mummy to the stand*

'As you can see, m'lord, the Countess is so injured that she is unable to answer any questions, but her very state is evidence of the great crime committed against her. I have no further questions.'

'Mr Nibble. Do you have any questions for the Countess?'

Willbury looked confused. 'Er . . . no, sir. Not if she cannot answer them.'

'Very well. Any more witnesses?'

'Yes, m'lord,' answered Smarmy Slingshot. 'Call Chadwick Spode.'

The police collected the Countess from the stand, and she was replaced by a small weeping man dressed in an emerald green and pink suit.

'Mr Spode. You are the fashion and society editor of the *Ratbridge Gazette*?'

The man nodded his head as he brushed tears away from his eyes with an orange hanky.

*He brushed tears away from his eyes with an orange hanky*

'Sir, speak up!' ordered the judge.

'I apologize on behalf of Mr Spode,' said Smarmy Slingshot, smirking at Willbury as he did so. 'He is in such distress that his doctor has given him orders not to speak, but he has prepared a statement for the court.'

Willbury stood. 'I object, m'lord. I have not been given a copy of this statement so have not been able to prepare questions based on it.'

'Mr Nibble! Objection denied. Given that he is medically excused from answering any questions I don't see it as necessary that you were given a copy. You are wasting my and the court's time and I will not take any further objections. Smarmy, please read the statement.'

Mr Smarmy Slingshot took a grubby piece of paper from the desk behind him and read.

*Mr Smarmy Slingshot took a grubby piece of paper from the desk*

'Dear court, yesterday afternoon I was working in my office when I heard of the huge disgrace that has been brought on the town. Ratbridge is a wonderful town and fine holiday destination, but it has been brought low by the criminal antics of the Nautical Laundry. How can visitors bring children here after hearing of the rude display of underwear, clearly visible from even several miles away. Our reputation is ruined. My social column in the paper will be a laughing stock. It may take years to recover from this outrage. Yours sincerely Chadwick Spode (GCSE English).'

Mr Spode was now weeping deeply into his hanky.

'M'lord, as you can see Mr Spode is sorely injured but this is nothing compared with the damage to the town's reputation. I ask that the court find the defendants guilty of all the charges and fine them an amount that will cover all damages.'

Judge Podger turned to Willbury. 'What have you got to say to that?'

'Sir, I would like to question the defendants.'

'I don't think so. How could we trust them? They will just give us some poppycock story.'

'I object, m'Lord!'

'I told you, Mr Nibble. No more objections or I will have you up for contempt of court. Any other witnesses?'

Willbury shook his head.

'Very well then. I order the jury to retire and bring back the verdict.' He then looked at his watch. 'You have three minutes!'

Willbury raised his hand. 'Sir, this really is outrageous! How can they make a fair judgement in just three minutes?'

*Willbury raised his hand*

'Silence, Mr Nibble. Given that the jury is made up from people of the town, I doubt very much that they will have any problem coming to the right verdict that quickly.'

Willbury was about to protest about the jury being likely to profit by a guilty verdict but as he opened his mouth to speak the judge cut him off.

'Just one word . . .' and Podger ran a finger across his throat.

The jury didn't even take one minute.

'How do you find the defendants?' the judge asked.

'Severely guilty on all and more charges!'

'Good!' Then Podger turned towards the dock.

'What you have done has injured both the town and the Countess. And you will be punished to the full extent of the law.' He turned to the clerk. 'What is that?'

'I'm not very good at sums . . .'

Mr Smarmy Slingshot stood. 'If I may help. I have done some calculations based on lost trade, wig repairs, personal injury, and the price of dignity. I reckon it is about ten thousand groats.'

There was a sharp intake of breath in the courtroom and even Judge Podger raised an eyebrow. Then he smiled.

'Sounds good to me. I fine the Ratbridge Nautical Laundry ten thousand groats.'

Willbury raised a hand.

'Yes, Mr Nibble?'

'My clients do not have such money.'

'Well, they had better find it.'

'Where, sir?'

'That is none of my business. I shall give them six months to find the funds, and if after that time they don't deliver I shall impose long prison sentences . . . or worse!'

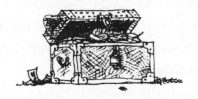

*Ten thousand groats*

*Titus and the boxtrolls turned and smiled at him*

# Chapter 4

# FINE!

At about the same time that the crew of the Nautical Laundry were walking out of the courtroom in a state of shock, Arthur was just emerging from his bedroom and creeping down the stairs. He'd been up very late. As he passed Grandfather's room he was tempted to check on the old man but there was a light snoring coming through the door so Arthur thought perhaps it would be better to leave his grandfather to sleep.

At the bottom of the stairs he crossed to the door to what had once been a pet shop, but now served as their living room and kitchen, as well as bedroom to Willbury and their friends Titus the cabbagehead, and Fish, Shoe, and Egg the boxtrolls. The door squeaked open and the familiar smell of bacon and cocoa hit his nose.

Titus and the boxtrolls turned and smiled at him, but he

could tell that they were worried.

'Have Willbury and Marjorie gone to the court?'

His friends nodded, and Fish, who was standing with a frying pan by the fire, pointed to some sausages and bacon in the pan.

'No thank you. I don't feel hungry.'

Fish pointed again and seemed insistent.

'Very well.' Arthur took a plate from Titus and held it out to Fish. Soon he was settled in an armchair eating while his friends sat about him and watched quietly.

Then steps and a key in the door broke the silence and Willbury entered. As he took the scarf from his neck he kicked the door closed, then turned to see Arthur and the creatures watching him.

'Sorry. It's just that damnable judge.' Then he looked upwards. 'Is your grandfather all right?'

'I think so,' said Arthur. 'I heard him snoring when I came downstairs. You're back very quickly. Have they delayed the case?'

'No. M'lord Podger has lived up to his reputation, and tried and sentenced in less than half an hour.'

'And?'

'He's fined them.'

'A fine. That's not too bad.'

'Ten thousand groats of not too bad!'

Arthur dropped his plate.

'Ten thousand groats!'

*'Is your grandfather all right?'*

Even the cabbagehead and boxtrolls understood this was a staggering amount of money and looked shocked.

'What are they going to do?'

'I have no idea but we'll get to that after we have sorted out Grandfather. Have you sent for the doctor?'

'No, I've only just got up.'

'Will you put on your shoes and go and fetch him?'

'I would . . . but are you sure he'd come? Grandfather threw him out last time after he turned up with leeches.'

*'He turned up with leeches.'*

'True . . . Maybe we should find another one, though they're all pretty useless.'

Titus, who had been listening intently, crept up to Willbury and pulled on his sleeve. Willbury looked down at him.

'What is it, Titus?'

The cabbagehead ran across the room to the barrel where he lived, popped inside, and reappeared with a copy of the *Ratbridge Gazette*. As he walked back across the room he opened the paper and searched for something. After scanning a few pages he found what he was looking for and held out the paper to Willbury.

Willbury took the paper and read aloud.

*Willbury took the paper and read aloud*

'"New Health Venture For All!
The people of Ratbridge will be
pleased to hear that a new doctor
(34) is to open a spa in our fair

metropolis. The great doctor goes
by the name of Doctor I. Snook
R. F. F. H. (28). Not only is this
great man (46) opening a spa but he
is going to offer free treatment to
all!"'

Willbury raised an eyebrow. 'That's not going to be
popular with quacks around here!'
Then he continued reading.

'"The Ratbridge Spa and
Alternative Therapy Centre is to
open on Saturday next and offer
the very latest in treatments for
the following illnesses—flu, the
common cold, athlete's foot,
tennis elbow, lice, measles,
housemaid's knee, and all that
ails the common man. And how is
this to be paid for, we ask? An
anonymous Ratbridge benefactor
(63?) is said to be behind the
scheme! When asked who this
philanthropic benefactor was, the
doctor (51) would only say that
the man was a retired local

businessman who felt that he wanted to pay back Ratbridge for all that he'd received from the town. Who could this be, we ask?

The Ratbridge Spa and Alternative Therapy Centre is to open in the refurbished buildings of the old Ratbridge public glue factory. And what treatments are we to expect? These the good doctor tells us are new, and fantastic, and based on a new remedy that he has formulated— a wonder drug that goes by the name of Black Jollop!

We here at the paper are not an easily impressed group of people and are ever watchful to protect the people of Ratbridge, so we sent one of our older hacks who happens to be blighted by gout, and often gets 'tired and emotional', to visit the new spa on a special pre-launch press day last week to try out the treatment for himself.

So did this Black Jollop fail to live up to the hype? Was our man left wanting?

 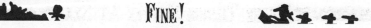

Quite frankly we were amazed! He came hopping back to our office (quite literally!) and took everybody down to the local hostelry to celebrate and to give a demonstration of his new-found health. Not only was he able to walk there unassisted, but after several refreshments he danced on the tables in a way that many younger colleagues were unable to match. Yes! This treatment really does work.

So we recommend that if you are sick of pills for your ills and leeches in your breeches, you hop off to the new Ratbridge Spa and Alternative Health Centre at the first chance."'

*He danced on the tables*

Willbury stopped reading. 'This all sounds rather too good to be true. But they've nothing to gain if they are not charging for it . . . Maybe we should try it.'

Then he looked back at the cover of the newspaper for a moment.

'It opened this morning!'

Arthur looked at Titus. 'Well done.'

Titus looked very happy that he had helped.

'What shall we do then?'

'I think we'd better go and wake Grandfather.'

They all trooped upstairs behind Willbury and entered Grandfather's bedroom. Grandfather was no longer asleep and looked at them from his bed.

'How are you doing this morning?'

*Grandfather was no longer asleep*

'Not well.'

'We think you should get some medical attention.'

'Not that terrible doctor . . . ' Grandfather protested weakly.

'No. There is a new spa with what sounds like a fantastic new treatment that the paper says really works.'

'Sounds like some money-making scheme.'

'No. They are not charging for treatment.'

Grandfather thought for a moment. 'Well, it might be worth a try.'

'So then we need to get you down there. Do you feel up to walking?'

Grandfather started to lift himself, then fell back on the bed. 'Not really.'

Fish the boxtroll gurgled to the other boxtrolls. They smiled and all disappeared.

'I wonder what they are up to?' said Willbury.

After a few minutes Fish came back to the bedroom and beckoned Arthur and Willbury to follow him. At the bottom of the stairs was a wheelbarrow filled with cushions and blankets.

'They've made him an ambulance!' exclaimed Arthur.

It took a few minutes to prepare Grandfather for his trip but soon they had him comfortably settled in his 'ambulance'. The boxtrolls very carefully lifted the handles and pushed it from the hall, through the shop and out into the street. Titus walked ahead checking for any potholes and signalled for the boxtrolls to manoeuvre to the left or right. As they got ever closer to the old glue factory it became increasingly busy with people, all hoping for a cure for some ill.

*Titus walked ahead*

*'Oh no! There's hundreds of them!'*

Chapter 5

# THE QUEUE

As Grandfather's barrow turned the corner of the lane that led to the old glue factory, it became clear just how many of the population of Ratbridge were seeking medical attention. The lane was crammed with the ill, injured, those who thought that they were, and some who were just worried about becoming so at a later date. Arthur looked in horror at the mass before them. There were those with bandages around various parts of their bodies, others were covered in spots and scabs, quite a few were supported by crutches, one man's nose had an angry-looking parrot attached to it and there were at least three children with their head stuck inside various pots and pans. It was not a pretty sight.

'Oh no! There's hundreds of them! We'll never get you treated, Grandfather!'

The journey had taken its toll on the old man and he was looking worse.

'What are we going to do?' Arthur moaned.

Around them the crowd was thickening and pushing them along.

'Stay together!' called Willbury.

Then some scuffling broke out quite near them. A large man with a brown paper bag tied around his head had tried to push past a group of old ladies, but they spotted him and set to work with their sticks and shopping bags in an attempt to drive him back. Another man thought he saw his chance in the distraction. He was in a self-propelled bath chair, and launched his transport at a small gap in the crowd. In doing so he managed to run over a bandaged gouty foot belonging to one of the town elders. There was a scream and more of the ill joined the scrap.

'Stay back!' warned Willbury. 'We must keep Grandfather safe!'

More and more of the crowd joined in the fighting.

*More and more of the crowd joined in the fighting*

Somewhat to Arthur's surprise it seemed to have a curative effect on a lot of the ill, with folks showing new-found vigour when facing queue jumping, or the chance to get ahead. A woman who was wrapped in bandages and had been lying on the ground moaning had jumped up and was now threatening to throttle anybody that tried to get past her with her dressings. Only by picking up the barrow and reversing out of the street did Arthur and his party avoid getting kicked or punched. The noise and commotion grew until it looked like a battle scene.

Then Arthur heard a loud whistle. He turned to look in the direction it came from and coming towards them were a large group of bicycle mounted policemen.

The Squeakers (as the policemen were locally known) threw down their bikes at the end of the street, and drew their truncheons.

'Riot positions!' ordered their officer. Immediately the Squeakers formed a line with truncheons raised high.

The officer blew his whistle as loudly as he could, and the sound reverberated off the walls of the lane, quieting the crowd.

'You lot have thirty seconds to form an orderly queue or you're in for a walloping!' he shouted.

The crowd didn't need a second warning. Immediately everyone stopped fighting and formed a neat line.

'I want a man every two yards along the street and if you see anybody try anything you have my full permission to . . . WALLOP!'

*The Squeakers with truncheons held high*

The Squeakers pushed down one side of the lane and took up their positions with truncheons still held high.

'What do we do now?' asked Arthur.

'Join the back of the queue?' offered Willbury.

'I suppose we'll have to, but it could take all day to get Grandfather seen.'

They took their place at the end of the line and began their wait. After a few minutes with no movement ahead of them Willbury spoke.

'I'll see if I can speed things up a bit.' He approached the Squeaker's officer who was still standing close by.

'Please. I have an old man with me who is really very ill and he needs to see a doctor right away!'

'Back in line!'

'But . . .'

'Back in line!'

'Please . . .'

Threateningly the officer raised his truncheon. Willbury backed off and returned to his friends.

'Looks like we'll have to wait our turn,' said Willbury.

Grandfather let out a pained moan. Arthur looked down at him and put a hand on Grandfather's forehead.

'He's very hot.'

'We've got to get you treated and soon. Most of this lot are wasting the doctor's time.'

Arthur was not sure that Willbury was being totally fair. There were a lot of people with fairly obvious illness and injuries, and after the fight there were even more, but he had to agree that it was urgent that his grandfather needed to see someone soon.

Looking at the queue he had an idea. 'I could try to sneak ahead, and get into the spa. Then I could ask if someone could see Grandfather straight away?'

Willbury looked around then whispered. 'I don't think that is going to be very easy. The Squeakers are on the lookout for that sort of thing.'

'I know. But we have to do something. I'm a lot smaller than most people here and if I got on my hands and knees I might be able to do it.'

Willbury looked at the crowd ahead of them. 'Do you really think you could do it without getting noticed?'

Arthur didn't feel sure he could, but he nodded.

'Very well. But I have an idea that might make it easier.' Willbury turned to Fish. 'Do you think you could make some very loud noise around the corner . . . as a distraction?'

Fish and the other boxtrolls gurgled to each other for a moment then Fish nodded.

'Well, you go off and get started; when we hear something Arthur can make his move.'

The boxtrolls scampered off and Arthur wondered what they were going to do.

While they waited for the boxtrolls to come up with something, Arthur tried to comfort Grandfather, then he noticed movement on the roof of the house opposite the end of the lane. A few seconds later he saw Fish's head pop up over the parapet and check the street below.

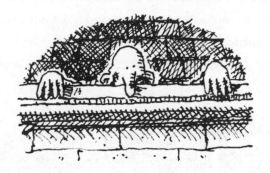

*Fish's head popped up over the parapet*

Then Fish disappeared and a moment later a large piece of guttering flew over the edge of the roof and dropped to the street.

CRASH!

*CRASH!*

The queue all turned towards the thunderous noise, and as they did Arthur dropped to his knees and slipped along the wall furthest from the Squeakers. He pushed himself between the people and the wall without them noticing and by the time the commotion had died away he was almost half the way down the queue. Around him everybody had returned to talking about their medical problems. As he huddled against the wall a man and woman directly in front of him were complaining about 'bad wind' and the 'vapours'. He made himself as small as he could and as the queue swayed a little he slid between them and the wall. Again he wasn't noticed.

*Arthur sneaked his way further and further forward*

Arthur sneaked his way further and further forward, now crawling on his hands and knees. As he made his way towards the spa he heard about every possible medical problem, and some that he thought were probably impossible. Everybody's infatuation with their own problems was all rather macabre, but meant that Arthur wasn't noticed.

He was only about twenty feet from the gates when he found himself behind a short, stout woman. His knees really hurt and he was dying to stand up, so he decided it was probably best to try and get to the front before he couldn't take any more. After a bit of thinking he came up with a plan.

*After a bit of thinking he came up with a plan*

Arthur had a piece of string in his pocket. He took it out and tied one end of it to the old lady's basket. He then passed the string around the right leg of the man standing behind him and then he crawled forward, while playing out the string. There was such a crush at the front of the queue that nobody noticed him scrabbling around at their feet amid the general jostle. Finally he reached a gap between the legs of people at the very front of the queue and the wall. He looked about. A policeman was standing by the gates and was signalling to the people at the front of the queue to enter the spa as soon as any patient came out. Arthur watched. When he saw the next patient coming out of the spa he waited until they reached the gates and he pulled hard on the string.

A scream came from behind. 'THIEF! Someone is trying to steal my bag!'

As everybody turned to look, Arthur made his move. He jumped up and walked past the policeman.

With all the confidence he could muster he spoke. 'It's my turn now.'

*The policeman just waved him through the gate*

The policeman, distracted by the commotion, just waved him through the gate.

Arthur picked up speed and made for the front doors of the spa. He reached the steps, swung the heavy door open and was greeted by a voice.

'Welcome to the Ratbridge Spa and Alternative Health Centre.'

*He swung the heavy door open*

*Two very slimy-looking men confronted Arthur*

Chapter 6

# TREATMENT

Two very slimy-looking men confronted Arthur. They were dressed in clothes that looked as if they had been stolen from a badly-dressed chef. And a very dirty chef too, for though the clothes might once have been white, they were now completely caked in filth.

'Can we 'elp you . . . sir?' asked one of them in an oily voice.

'Yes. My grandfather's really ill and needs help. Quickly!'

'Where is 'e then?'

'In the queue.'

'Well 'e'll have to wait his turn.'

'You don't understand. He is really ill.'

'Did you hear that, Nurse Puggly? Tragic!'

Nurse Puggly was giving Arthur a funny look.

'Are you the young *gent* what lives with all them creatures and the old lawyer?'

*'Are you the young gent what lives with
all them creatures and the old lawyer?'*

'Yes. Why?' Arthur felt uneasy. How did the nurse know who he was?

'It's of no matter,' replied Nurse Puggly. He turned to his companion and spoke very firmly. 'Think we can make an exception here. Be tragic if one of this poor lad's friends was to get away . . . without treatment. We better take the young man to see the good doctor.'

*A large hand took hold of Arthur's shoulder*

A large hand took hold of Arthur's shoulder and he found himself being marched abruptly into the spa. Arthur felt confused for a moment, but the main thing was that he was on his way to see the doctor. Perhaps he would get Grandfather treated in time after all.

They reached the 'ward', and while his guards went to find the doctor, Arthur looked about what had once been the boiling room of the old glue factory. He was not sure but it looked as if very little had changed since the days of glue production. Large metal vats still occupied most of the floor space and pipe-work criss-crossed between them. The only concession to its new purpose was iron bedsteads filling every gap and absolutely everything had been badly painted a sickly pale green.

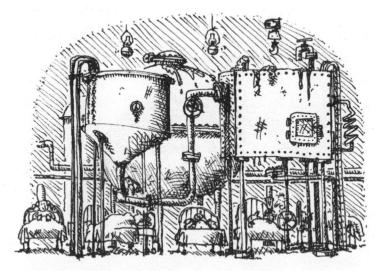

*The only concession to its new purpose was iron bedsteads filling every gap*

The only colour in the ward was the staff and the patients on the beds (and some of them were pretty green too). At the other end of the ward a crowd of the nurses were gathered about what Arthur guessed was the doctor—a very tall man pronouncing loudly about some patient who was hidden amongst the crowd. Even from where Arthur stood he could hear the diagnosis.

*A very tall man pronouncing*

'This is a case of terminal halitosis, and as you can see, the patient is in the latter stages of the disease. He would shortly go downhill and kick the bucket were I not to administer treatment. And does anybody have any idea of what sort of treatment we should give for such a condition?'

With one cry the nurses surrounding him shouted 'BLACK JOLLOP!'

'Correct. Hold him down!'

There were some muffled cries and then silence. After a minute or so the doctor broke the silence.

'There! What did I tell you? See! The colour is coming

back to his cheeks and the stench is disappearing!'

The crowd started to clap.

'Thank you, thank you. I know, I know! I just can't keep all this talent to myself. It just wouldn't be right. Now release the patient and send him on his way.'

The crowd opened to reveal the patient. Arthur could see the man smiling and watched as he tested his new breath on one of the nurses. This had no effect on the nurse and the man's smile broadened.

'I's cured!' shrieked the patient as he skipped past Arthur towards the exit.

'Who's next?' called the doctor.

*He tested his new breath on one of the nurses*

Arthur felt the hand on his shoulder tighten.

'Doctor! We have a lad here whose grandfather is in desperate need of attention.'

'Can't you see I have lots more patients waiting in the beds?'

'I think this might be more important. The governor

might be rather interested in making sure it happens.'

The doctor made his way over to Arthur and looked him up and down.

'What's special about him?'

*'What's special about him?'*

The nurse holding Arthur's shoulder leant over and whispered something in the doctor's ear. After a few moments the doctor raised an eyebrow.

'I think we must see what we can do then.' The doctor turned to Arthur. 'Well, lead us to your poor grandfather. We shall see what we can do.'

Again Arthur felt a strong sense of unease sweeping over him. He had never seen any of these people before, but they seemed to be singling him out for special treatment. Perhaps

it was just that they could see how very worried he was about his grandfather, and wanted to help him.

Arthur led the group out through the doors of the spa and back on to the street. The queue was waiting impatiently and when they saw the doctor there was a surge forward.

The doctor started to panic, then spotting one of the Squeakers he called out, 'Keep order! There's a very sick man out there that we need to get to.'

Several Squeakers came forward and raised their truncheons to make the queue part. Under the Squeakers' protection Arthur and the doctor's group made their way up the street to the place where Grandfather and the others were waiting. Willbury saw them approaching and was looking very worried.

'Not a moment too soon. He's had a turn for the worse.'

In the barrow Grandfather had his eyes closed and was shivering as Titus mopped the old man's brow with a cabbage leaf. Fish and the other boxtrolls were standing by the barrow and looking panicked.

'This is my grandfather,' said Arthur, pointing.

The doctor took a very quick look and spoke.

'Just as I suspected. In need of urgent treatment! Bring him straight to the main ward and I'll sort him out.'

Willbury came forward. 'I'm very thankful, sir. May we come with you?'

'Certainly. Wouldn't want the patient to be lonely, would

we?' the doctor replied. With this he turned back towards the spa and set off at high speed.

Brushing the others away the nurses picked the barrow clean off the ground and followed the doctor. Willbury took Arthur's hand.

'Well done. I didn't think you'd manage it. How did you convince them?'

'I'm not quite sure. They just seemed to want to come and help. Maybe they could just tell it was serious.'

'Wonderful! The doctor really must care.'

On reaching the spa the nurses had to lower the barrow to avoid banging Grandfather on the top of the doorway. As they reached the ward Arthur noticed that Willbury seemed rather surprised.

'Isn't it inconvenient having all this old equipment in here amongst the beds?' said Willbury, addressing the doctor.

'Quite the reverse,' replied the doctor. 'We need it for processing my wondrous cure.'

'In glue vats?'

'We did wash them!' The doctor seemed quite put out. Then he instructed the nurses to place Grandfather in a bed. There didn't seem to be an empty one so the nurses pushed an old lady with spots out of the nearest one and told her to find somewhere else.

'Are you sure that is necessary?' asked Willbury. The woman did look ill.

'Nothing is too much for such an urgent case,' replied the doctor.

There was a clearing in the centre of the ward between the biggest of the vats and in it were a large number of patients standing before a desk. Behind the desk were more nurses, this time with clipboards and spoons. Arthur watched as the attendants dispensed a dose of some foul-looking syrup from the barrel and gave it to another old lady at the front of the queue. She took the spoon in her mouth, made a horrid face and was about to spit it out when one of the attendants pinched her lips around the spoon and looked menacing.

'Swallow up!'

*One of the attendants pinched her lips around the spoon*

The old lady did as she was told. Then the attendant took his hands and the spoon away from her mouth and pointed her towards a bed.

'Lie down for ten minutes and you'll be feeling better.'

It was all the old lady could do to keep from bringing the medicine up, but she settled back on the bed with her hand over her mouth.

'Now . . . treatment!' said the doctor as he cast an eye over Grandfather. 'Fetch the jollop. Two spoonfuls I think. Nurses . . . hold him down!'

'Hold him down?' Willbury looked shocked.

'Powerful stuff, Black Jollop! The human body does not always know what's good for it.'

Grandfather tried to sit up but before he could move nurses descended upon him. Then the nurse with the spoon collected a dose from the barrel and came forward. As the spoon came closer a foul smell filled the air. Whatever it was, it had more than a little of the boiled cabbage about it, only worse.

'Oh God!' muttered Grandfather. 'Do I have to?'

'I think you must, sir!'

Grandfather opened his mouth and the first spoonful shot in. His face went white as he swallowed and he opened again. 'I think I would rather be . . . '

But before he could get the words out, a second spoon appeared and shot into his mouth. A nurse quickly pinched Grandfather's lips closed.

'How long will it take in a case like this?' asked Willbury.

The doctor smiled. 'Oh, you'd be surprised.'

'How are you feeling?' asked Arthur.

Grandfather reluctantly swallowed and the nurse released his grip.

'I'm not sure. There is a very strange feeling in my stomach . . . and it's spreading out from there . . . '

A smile broke out on Grandfather's face. 'IT WORKS! It really works!'

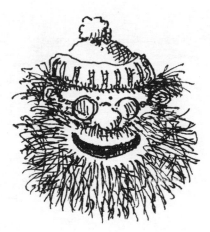

*'IT WORKS! It really works!'*

'What do you mean?' asked Arthur.

'I can feel the pain in my chest going.'

They all watched as Grandfather sat up and lifted himself from the bed. Arthur went to help, but Grandfather ushered him away. 'Let me do it. Do you know what? Not only have the pains in my chest gone but my hips feel better than they have for years. Remarkable!'

Grandfather lifted one leg from the floor and took a hop.

'Steady on, old man. Go easy!' said Willbury.

'It's fine. I feel fabulous.' With that Grandfather did a little dance. Everybody apart from the doctor was amazed. Grandfather tried a kick in the air and to his surprise his leg almost kicked Willbury's nose.

*His leg almost kicked Willbury's nose*

'I haven't been able to do that for years.'

'Take it easy!' ordered Willbury. 'You could injure yourself . . . or me.'

Arthur was overjoyed. He had never seen his grandfather like this, and joined in the dance.

'Dancing ain't allowed in the spa,' snapped one of the nurses.

The dancing stopped and Grandfather looked at the doctor.

'Sir, I want to thank you from the bottom of my heart.'

The doctor looked very pleased with himself. 'Not a problem. It would be churlish to keep all this talent to myself.'

'And coming out to fetch me before treating all the others.'

'When I heard you were connected with the lad I insisted that we give you top priority. It would be our benefactor's wish.'

Willbury looked puzzled. 'Your benefactor? Who's he?'

The doctor looked sheepish. 'A local businessman who wishes to remain anonymous. He's always felt that he wanted to pay back Ratbridge for what he's received from the town so he aids me with my research and with the funding for this fine spa.'

*The doctor looked sheepish*

'If he wanted us to have priority, as you say, he must know us, and presumably we know him.'

'Shall we just say that he has run across you in the past and believes you are deserving of special treatment. Beyond that I will say nothing.' The doctor put his finger to his lips and then smiled.

'Then will you pass along our thanks to him,' said Willbury.

'Of course, but do remember—it is I who have created this wonderful treatment.'

The doctor seemed a little put out that he was not getting enough praise.

'Of course, we cannot thank you enough, but do pass a little of the thanks on.'

'I shall. But now I really must get on, there are many others deserving of treatment.'

With that the doctor turned his back on the group and made off to the next case.

Arthur looked over at Grandfather who was smiling.

'He is a very odd man, and though he seems to have cured you I can't warm to him.'

'Great men are often a little strange. Never mind. Let's get off home and celebrate. I feel wonderful!'

The friends set off. This time Arthur rode in the wheelbarrow pushed by the boxtrolls. In the street outside they got some very envious looks from the queue, but Arthur didn't care. His grandfather was well again.

When they reached home Willbury disappeared and then returned with a packet of some rather special cocoa that he'd been saving for Christmas.

'This calls for a celebration. Fetch the bucket!'

*'This calls for a celebration. Fetch the bucket!'*

*Jumping about like newborn lambs*

## Chapter 7

# FIXED!

'I wonder if they'd give me a drop of that Black Jollop for my knees. They get a bit stiff when it's damp,' Willbury was musing over his cocoa. Fish and Shoe also seemed interested in treatment and gurgled while pointing to various parts of their anatomy.

'One drop of that stuff and you'll all be jumping about like newborn lambs. Get yourself down there first thing tomorrow,' said Grandfather.

Willbury shook his head. 'Better leave it to those in real need.'

The boxtrolls looked disappointed.

'I think we could go for a walk this afternoon to test my hips and to let the crew of the laundry know I'm all right.'

'And to check on how they are doing,' added Willbury.

The mention of the laundry brought everyone back down to earth.

'Is there anything you can do for them?' Grandfather asked.

'I might be able to appeal against the fine but I doubt I will be successful. Judge Podger is well in with the Law Lords and they are very unlikely to go against him.'

They set off to the Nautical Laundry in sombre mood. Grandfather did manage a few smiles along the way, but the thought of their friends' troubles spoilt the relief of Grandfather's recovery.

'He's all right!' came a cry from the bridge. Kipper had spotted them and had seen that Grandfather was recovered.

Soon the whole crew assembled to greet them and listened to the story of the Black Jollop.

'We were so worried,' said Kipper. 'That stuff sounds like a miracle.'

*'That stuff sounds like a miracle.'*

'It is indeed,' answered Grandfather. 'And I thank you for your concern, but you have troubles of your own.'

'Yes . . . ' replied Kipper and the crew suddenly looked very glum.

'Have you come up with any ideas as to how you could pay the fine?'

'Only one. We could sell the ship.'

'SELL YOUR SHIP!' Arthur looked appalled. 'But you are pirates. You can't sell your ship.'

'I think we will have to.'

'And even then we would be lucky to get as much as half of the money, so we would end up in prison in any case,' added Tom.

'We could do a runner?' suggested Bert.

'We have told you no already, Bert. We are not cut out for a life on the run and besides I think they would notice us trying to get the ship unstuck from the canal.'

'So . . . ' asked Arthur. 'What next?'

*'What next?'*

*Quite a lot of arm wrestling*

## Chapter 8

# AN OFFER

Grandfather and his new-found health took some getting used to and soon everybody apart from Grandfather was worn out. There had been walks, a visit to the swimming pool, dancing, and quite a lot of arm wrestling (which the boxtrolls enjoyed). Arthur noticed one other change in his grandfather—he'd lost his sweet tooth. In the past if cake or sweets were ever around Grandfather was never far behind. But now when cocoa and buns came out, Grandfather refused them.

'What's up with you?'

'I think it's my body telling me to eat well. I just don't fancy anything sweet since I got better. It's odd but I do have a desire for something, but I just can't put my finger on what it is. I'm sure it will come to me.'

Later that night Grandfather awoke in a sweat. As he sat

up in bed he found himself sniffing the air. There was a faint trace of whatever it was he couldn't remember earlier. He still couldn't put a name to it, but he found himself licking his lips as he settled down to sleep again. By his bed a pair of very muddy slippers sat in a small puddle.

Over breakfast the following morning Arthur noticed Grandfather looked preoccupied, but he snapped out of it when Arthur caught his eye and smiled.

'I am not sure why it is but I feel a little tired this morning. I have a feeling that . . . ' But before Grandfather could go on there was a rapping at the front door. Arthur answered it and was rather surprised to see the doctor standing on the doorstep.

'Can I help?' asked Arthur.

'I'd like to speak to my patient and that lawyer chappie.'

*The doctor standing on the doorstep*

Arthur ushered the doctor into the shop and Willbury and the others stood to greet their guest.

'Welcome, doctor. Come to check up on your patient?' said Willbury with an outstretched hand.

This seemed to perplex the doctor but he nodded and shook Willbury's hand.

'Er . . . yes. How is he doing?'

'Very well, thank you.'

'Good. And I've come to ask for help.'

'Help?' asked Grandfather.

'Yes, help. Just like I gave you.'

'Of course. Whatever we can do.'

'The demand for Black Jollop is far higher than I ever imagined. Frankly, it is running out.'

'Oh dear.' Grandfather looked very concerned. 'You had better make some more.'

'That is the problem. It's not quite that easy. I need a certain ingredient and it's almost all gone. It is not a thing one can just get hold of. That is where you're to help. If I am to continue my good work you have to help me with some importing.'

Arthur thought this sounded a bit pushy.

'What can we do? We're not importers of anything,' replied Willbury.

'I am coming to that. I understand you're very good friends of the crew of that ship on the canal. I need them to make a trip.'

'So what do you want us to do?'

'They're your friends, aren't they? Get down there and tell them they are off on a voyage.'

'But . . . '

'Look here. I may well have saved this gentleman's life,' said the doctor, pointing rather rudely at Grandfather. 'Are you going to let me down when I need you?'

'No . . . no,' said Grandfather. 'It is just that it is not our ship, and they have troubles of their own.'

'This is a major emergency and if you let me down you'll not just be letting me down but also the people of Ratbridge.'

'I understand, but asking them to go on a voyage . . . '

'I'd think that it is the very least you could do for me considering that you might have died.'

There was a pause then Grandfather spoke.

'Very well. I'll ask them. But I'm not sure they can help us. Didn't you hear what happened to them in court?'

'Yes I did indeed. Sounded like they might be at a loose end now anyway.'

Willbury spoke up. 'And to where would this voyage be?'

'That is a secret. I have to closely guard the formula of Black Jollop. I'll provide someone to go on the voyage who'll know the destination.'

'The Ratbridge Nautical Laundry has to find money to pay off their fine, so why would they ever agree to going on a journey?'

*'I have to closely guard the formula of Black Jollop.'*

'To help you, the people of Ratbridge—and to earn ten thousand groats.'

'TEN THOUSAND GROATS!'

'My backer is so keen to spread the benefits of Black Jollop that he's willing to put up the money.'

'What do you think?' Grandfather asked Willbury. This seemed the answer to everybody's problems.

*'TEN THOUSAND GROATS!'*

'Seems more than generous.' Willbury turned to the doctor.

'How would we know that you would come through with the money?'

'Really! After all I have done for you. But what do you expect from a lawyer? Don't worry. I have a contract.'

The doctor pulled out a document from his inside pocket and passed it to Willbury.

*The doctor pulled out a document from his*
*inside pocket and passed it to Willbury*

'It basically says that the ship and its crew will fetch supplies and in return shall receive the sum of ten thousand groats on return to Ratbridge.'

Willbury inspected the document.

'That is what it says. Also it hands captaincy and control of the ship over to you, though.'

'Technically that may be true, but my lawyers are insisting on it. If we are paying that much money we want control. The crew will be more than generously compensated for it. If they can do without the money . . . '

'I think we had better go and ask them. It's a lot of money.'

'Good. I shall expect to hear from you shortly. By ten-ish tomorrow morning if possible.'

With that, the doctor walked to the door. 'Supplies are running very short and there is already a queue outside the spa for when we open tomorrow. I must go and prepare myself to turn away the sick.'

The door closed.

*It took even less time for them to agree*

## Chapter 9

# FIREWORKS

It didn't take long to tell the crew about the contract and it took even less time for them to agree. Ten thousand groats was exactly enough to get the crew of the Ratbridge Nautical Laundry to sign the contract. There were still a few problems—how to free the ship from where she was stuck, the fact they were facing the wrong direction in the canal with no space to turn round, and how to provision the ship. Marjorie thought she had answers to the first two problems.

'I think there are three methods we could use to un-stick her. One: Pull her out. Two: Dismantle the bridge by hand. Three: Something a bit more interesting.' She smiled.

'What is the "something a bit more interesting"?'

'It's the most elegant and least tiring one.'

'What?'

'Wait for this evening. I could be ready by then . . . if I'm allowed to help myself to the stores.'

'Of course! Would you like any help?' offered Tom.

'No, I think I will be able to manage it on my own.'

'And what about the fact the ship is facing the wrong way up the canal?' asked Tom.

'Simple,' answered Kipper. 'Use the engine. It will drive us backwards, won't it, Marjorie?'

'Yes. All we have to do is put one more pulley in the drive train and she will go backwards all day. Might look a bit strange, going backwards down the canal. But once we get to somewhere we can turn round I can take the pulley back out and we can go forwards again.'

'Brilliant!' said Kipper.

Marjorie winked and disappeared below decks with a smile on her face. Tom then got out the chest where they kept their money and counted it up. It totalled eight groats and would barely cover a week's shopping, let alone provisions for an entire voyage.

*Marjorie winked*

'I'm not sure what we are going to do? Does anybody have any savings tucked away?'

After a few minutes the crew returned with another twelve groats in loose change, but it was still nothing like enough.

Willbury then came to their aid. 'I'll lend you the money on one condition. That I can come along!'

'Certainly!' smiled Tom. 'We would be more than happy to have you along.'

'Well I have one hundred and twenty-five groats invested at the post office—but it is my life savings and I really will need it back.'

The crew gave him a cheer.

'Do you know how soon the doctor wants us to set off?'

'As soon as possible.'

'When would it be possible to get your money?'

'All I have to do is get my pass book from home.'

'Would you like some of us to come along as guards?' asked Kipper. 'It is an awful lot of money.'

'Yes please.'

'Blunderbusses?' offered Bert.

*A Blunderbuss*

'I think that would draw attention to us and might also be highly illegal.'

'Shall I bring my cosh?'

'Very well. But you are not to bring it out unless someone else starts trouble.'

Bert agreed and Willbury set off with most of the crew in tow. As they walked they drew up a list of everything they would need for a long voyage.

*As they walked they drew up a list*

\* \* \*

'Ready!' Marjorie shouted. It was early evening and after a busy day everybody was gathered on the towpath to watch. Marjorie ushered the spectators back behind a barrier she had erected some distance down the towpath, then she walked back to the bridge.

From where Arthur was standing he could see long sticks, each with a tube at the top, protruding from all over the bridge.

'I wonder what she is up to?'

'I am very sure we are going to find out, and very shortly,' smiled Grandfather.

*Marjorie ushered the spectators back behind a barrier*

Willbury was looking uneasy.

Then Marjorie came back towards the spectators, reeling out something as she did.

'What's going to happen?' Arthur asked.

'Watch!'

She pulled a box of matches from her pocket and leant down to the ground where the end of the string she had been reeling out lay. Then she struck a match and held it to the end of the string. After a few splutters the string caught light and there was a fizzling and a sparking as the fire rapidly moved along the string towards the bridge.

'A fuse! You're not blowing up the bridge are you?' shouted Willbury in horror.

'Wait and see!' she chuckled.

The sparkling reached the first of the sticks and things started to happen.

'Watch!' cried Marjorie in delight.

With a stream of flame one of the sticks shot high into the sky, then its jet fizzled out.

*This was followed by another and another*

This was followed by another and another. Some of the 'rockets' seemed at first to struggle to get off the ground, but slowly they all managed to disappear into the night sky. The display went on for minutes, slowly enveloping the bridge in a thick cloud of smoke. As it died away Willbury spoke.

'Very nice, Marjorie! Fireworks! But what about the bridge?'

'Wait until the smoke clears.'

Arthur watched. The huge plume of smoke started to drift off in the wind.

THE BRIDGE WAS GONE!

The applause died away and Marjorie bowed.

'Simple really. The rockets were fixed to all the stones that made up the bridge and POOF! Redistribution!'

Willbury looked rather unhappy, but not as unhappy as all the gardeners with greenhouses in Ratbridge were the following morning.

Arthur congratulated her. 'You're brilliant, Marjorie! There is nothing to stop us setting sail now.'

Willbury and Grandfather both looked at him, then at each other.

*Not as unhappy as all the gardeners with greenhouses
in Ratbridge were the following morning*

'I'm sorry, Arthur, but you are too young to go on this trip. You're going to have to stay here with me,' said Grandfather.

Arthur suddenly felt as though his world had collapsed. All day he'd been imagining setting off with his friends on the adventure and now in a moment it had been taken away from him.

'But Grandfather . . . '

'I'm sorry, I have discussed it with Willbury and he is of the opinion that this really isn't the sort of thing a lad of your age should be involved in.'

'Grandfather . . . '

'Arthur, that is an end to it.'

Arthur looked about at his friends the pirates and rats. They looked disappointed as well, but were keeping quiet.

'Maybe when you are older,' said Willbury.

This was the final straw. Arthur turned and walked away down the towpath.

*Arthur turned and walked away down the towpath*

*Those cheeses that escaped made for the woods*

## Chapter 10

# AN OUTRAGE!

The sky was clouded and the moon threw almost no light on the boggy marshes where the cheeses slept. The gentle but rather stupid creatures were slowly rebuilding their numbers after almost being wiped out in the days of cruel cheese hunting. Now of course that barbaric practice was banned. The sound of the water from the river mixed with the snoring of the cheeses, and masked the soggy footsteps of the approaching predators.

Then there was a crazed yell and the attack upon the innocent creatures started. From the darkness human shapes appeared and ran towards the panicking cheeses. The startled creatures took flight. But only the more mature cheeses knew the ground and were fast enough to evade the onslaught. As for the young and weak . . . there was little hope.

Those cheeses that escaped made for the woods, but were followed by the evil humans who'd been too slow to feast on the early victims. Soon these hunters were wandering about in the darkness amongst the trees, bumping into things and whimpering with their unfulfilled cheese lust. The trembling, terrified cheeses quivered in their hiding places behind trees and down burrows. After several desperate hours of searching the baying mob gave up and turned back towards the town, needing to get back to their beds before the night was over.

As the sun rose a lonely woman now reduced to doing her own washing settled a basket by the riverbank and looked about to find a suitable rock to scrub her clothes on. Her eyes fell upon something yellow, bobbing in the shallows. She reached down and picked it up. Turning it slowly in her hand, she began to shiver.

As she fell to the ground in a faint, her lips mouthed a word.

'RIND . . . '

*Turning it slowly in her hand, she began to shiver*

*Titus looked a little shocked*

## Chapter 11

# READY FOR THE OFF

Fish was standing by his usual place at the fire cooking breakfast when Arthur made his way down to the front room of the old shop. The boxtrolls and Titus were gurgling to each other excitedly, which made Arthur feel worse. When Fish held out the sausages Arthur shook his head and went to sit in Willbury's chair. For a few moments the boxtrolls went quiet but soon they started to gurgle on again. Titus offered Arthur a plate.

'Leave me alone!'

Titus looked a little shocked but backed off.

Then Fish came over and tried to console Arthur.

'Grumfff greee?'

Arthur pushed his hand away.

Fish pointed up the stairs and signalled Arthur to fetch Grandfather and Willbury for breakfast. Arthur lifted himself out of the chair and clumped up the stairs. He was about to enter Grandfather's room when he heard talking and stopped.

*He heard talking and stopped*

'I know Arthur really wants to go, but he really is too young.' It was Willbury.

'Yes, but they take eight-year-olds into the navy!'

'And look how they are treated! No! It'll never do. As his guardian you've a responsibility to look after him, and allowing him to go off on that wreck of a ship to some undefined destination is just not on. Imagine if something went wrong. How would you feel?'

'I know, I know . . . but you could keep an eye on him.'

Arthur was shocked. His grandfather would allow him to go. It was Willbury who was stopping it happening.

'Besides, who would look after you if you fell ill again?'

'I am sure I'll be fine—but if I took a turn for the worse I could find someone. We broke Arthur's heart last night when we told him he couldn't go. The experience might even be good for him.'

'Never! He's just too young.'

'Maybe if . . .'

'No! And let that be an end to it.'

Arthur heard Willbury making for the door and so rushed to make his way back down the stairs and sit down in the armchair again. This time when Fish passed him a plate of eggs and bacon, he reluctantly took it and started to eat.

*He reluctantly took it and started to eat*

'Ah Arthur! Just the person I wanted to see.' It was Willbury. 'Kipper and Tom dropped by earlier to tell me that the ship is ready. I want you to go down and tell the doctor.'

Arthur felt the food stick in his throat. He swallowed hard and didn't answer.

'Arthur. I want you to go down to the doctor to tell him the ship is ready!'

'All right,' muttered Arthur.

'Good,' said Willbury, then turning to the boxtrolls he added, 'Apparently they've made me up a real sailor's hammock.'

'You're going to have to muck in a bit with the crew,' replied Grandfather.

'I'm sure I can manage. I've never been to sea before. I'm looking forward to it.'

This was too much for Arthur and he put his plate down and headed for the front door. As he laced up his boots Willbury was telling Grandfather what the pirates had told him of their old voyages. Arthur felt sick. As he let himself out he heard Willbury telling of islands where giant tortoises lived, and others where there were huge birds that tasted delicious and you could just pick them up and put them in a cooking pot.

Arthur slammed the door.

*Huge birds that tasted delicious*

*A large notice was fixed to the gates*

# Chapter 12
# CAST OFF!

When Arthur reached the spa there was no queue. A large notice was fixed to the gates. 'Closed. We are unable to treat patients due to a lack of Black Jollop.'

He pushed open the gate and made his way across the deserted courtyard, through the main doors, and down the corridor to the main ward. The doctor was standing alone behind a desk stacked with strange equipment and seemed very preoccupied.

Arthur watched for a moment then coughed. This startled the doctor who looked up, quickly came around the desk, and placed himself between Arthur and the apparatus on the desk.

'What do you want? We're closed.'

'The ship's ready.'

'Good! Tell them I'll be along this afternoon. Now get out of here!'

Arthur turned away but noticed the doctor was following him. As soon as he passed through the gates the doctor closed and bolted them behind him. Arthur found himself alone again and feeling really miserable.

What now? he thought to himself. He couldn't face going back to the shop and in truth he was very curious to see how things were getting on at the ship. He decided to head for the canal.

The sight of the ship made his heart sink further. There had been a transformation. All its woodwork had been either washed or painted, sails had been taken out of storage and bound to the spars, new rigging had been put up, and the crew were now busy polishing, scrubbing or stowing things away. The ship no longer looked like a laundry. It looked like a vessel ready for the high seas.

*There had been a transformation*

'Arthur! I've got something for you,' Marjorie shouted from the stern deck.

He looked up.

'What is it?'

Marjorie looked a little furtive and pulled out something on a chain.

'The key for the submarine. I've put a padlock on the hatch to stop anybody messing about with her while we're away. I want you to keep an eye on her.'

*Something on a chain*

She threw the key down to him and Arthur caught it and put it in his pocket. The weight of it reminded him that he was not going.

'Did you tell the doctor we're ready?'

He silently nodded.

'Did he say when he was going to get here?'

'No. Just later this afternoon.'

'I guess he'll just turn up.' With that she turned and set about oiling something. Arthur sat down on the bank and watched the clamour. After a while he looked across to the submarine. There could not be a greater difference between

the two craft. One looked full of life and the other old and dismal. Though he was now in charge of the submarine he really couldn't care less if it sank. He turned away from it and stared back at the ship.

What could he do? He had to get on the voyage. He stood and slowly crept up the gangplank, looking about. On one side of the mast was a large barrel. He walked over to it and lifted the lid. It was absolutely full of apples.

'Not thinking of becoming a stowaway, are we?'

He turned to see Willbury looking down at him. Arthur didn't reply.

'Don't think you can get away with any funny stuff. I shall be keeping an eye out for you, and making sure you're not aboard.'

Arthur dropped the lid of the barrel, and walked sulkily across the deck, down the gangplank, and off in the direction of the shop.

*Off in the direction of the shop*

At four the doctor arrived on a cart pulled by a very exhausted donkey. He insisted on being taken to the captain's cabin where he installed himself with his luggage. This consisted of about twenty very large trunks and cases. It took quite a lot of effort by some of the largest pirates to get them on deck, and down below. Though exhausted, the pirates offered to help him unpack but the doctor refused.

*A cart pulled by a very exhausted donkey*

'Don't worry. They contain delicate equipment I need for the jollop. I shall unpack them tonight.'

He then asked for the key to the cabin and locked it before joining the crew on deck.

Word had got around about the voyage and a crowd was starting to assemble to see the ship set off.

About six o'clock Grandfather heard a newspaper boy calling out in the street.

'Late edition! Late edition! Ship about to set sail! Black Jollop Voyage Special! Read all about it!'

*'Late edition! Late edition!'*

Grandfather went up and found Arthur in his bedroom.

'They'll be setting off shortly. Shall we go and wave goodbye?'

Arthur shook his head.

'Very well. You stay here then.'

'Why can't I go?'

'I've told you. You're not old enough to take care of yourself.'

'Who was it that helped save you in the submarine?'

' . . . you . . . '

'And last year who was it that saved the town from Snatcher and his men?'

' . . . you . . . '

'So I'm old enough to look after others but not old enough to take care of myself then?'

'I know it seems rough . . . ' But before Grandfather could finish Arthur started again.

'So be truthful with me. How would you feel if you were my age and there was a real adventure about to happen and your grandfather stopped you from going?'

Grandfather thought for a few moments. 'Not very good, but I am only trying to protect you.'

'I remember you telling me loads of times that we learn from experience. And now you want to stop me from learning?'

'Of course not.'

'How old does the navy take boys?'

'Eight, I think.'

'Well, I'm ten. Perhaps I should run away and join the navy?'

'No! God knows what would happen to you if you did.'

'So it would be better if I learnt from people who cared for me, like Tom and Kipper?'

'I suppose so.'

'SO I CAN GO?'

'I didn't say that.'

'But can I?'

Grandfather looked the boy up and down. It was true that Arthur had already done much a man twice his age would have been proud of.

'You mean the world to me, Arthur. I couldn't bear it if I lost you.'

'You won't.'

'Please, please be careful.'

Arthur looked up him. 'What do you mean?'

'If you really want to go on this voyage . . . you go.'

*'If you really want to go on this voyage . . . you go.'*

'Do you really mean it? What about Willbury?'

'I'm your guardian, not Willbury. It might even be good for you. What is life without adventure?'

Arthur could not believe what had just been said. He grabbed a sack from the corner of the room and threw his clothes in.

'Better be quick! They could be going any minute.'

'Are you going to be all right without me?'

'Don't you worry about me. Let's get down there quick.'

Arthur rushed down the stairs three at a time, with Grandfather following. Even with Grandfather's new-found health and the fact that Arthur was having to carry quite a large sack, Grandfather was having trouble keeping up. Through the shop, out into the streets and towards the canal they ran. As they got closer the crowds started to hinder their progress, and they noticed something. The crowd were not going towards the mooring. They were coming away.

'Quick! They must have set sail,' Arthur called back to Grandfather. Then he reached the towpath and looked towards where the ship had lain. There stood the boxtrolls, but there was no trace of the ship—just the ruined remains of the bridge. Arthur followed the gaze of the boxtrolls along the canal.

In the far distance he could just make out a faint plume of smoke. They had gone!

*Fish held up a finger and turned it in a circle*

## Chapter 13

# SUNK!

'How long ago did they leave?'

Fish held up a finger and turned it in a circle.

'An hour ago?' Arthur panted.

Fish nodded.

Disappointment filled Arthur's heart and the tears started to well up in his eyes. The boxtrolls shook their heads, and Arthur started to feel sick. He put a hand in his pocket to reach for his hanky—and touched upon the key chain. He pulled out the key and looked at the submarine.

'I can catch them up . . . I'll use the submarine.'

'You can't. That thing will only get stuck again,' replied Grandfather.

'Not if I keep on the surface.'

'But you'll never be able to operate it on your own.'

'I'll need help then.' Arthur looked towards the boxtrolls.

Fish, Shoe, and Egg all took a step back.

'Please, please, I know you hate water but this is the chance of a lifetime for me.'

Arthur saw something in Fish's eyes glimmer for a moment.

'Fish, will you help me? You don't have to come to sea, just help me get it started. You boxtrolls are brilliant with machines.'

Fish was looking very nervous, but took a gulp, then a step forward, and nodded.

Arthur grinned from ear to ear, while the other boxtrolls looked horrified.

'Come on then!' Arthur jumped on to the roof and unlocked the hatch. Reluctantly Fish stepped over the gap, and hung on to Arthur. As soon as the hatch was open Arthur pushed the Boxtroll up and into the tower.

*Fish stepped over the gap, and hung on to Arthur*

'You go steady my boy, and take care!' called Grandfather from the bank as Arthur climbed in after Fish.

'I will. And you look after yourself,' Arthur beamed back. 'Cast off . . . please.'

With the aid of the remaining Boxtrolls, Grandfather freed the submarine and waved them off.

Inside, Fish seemed a little happier. It was bone dry, warm, and the smell of oil settled him. After looking about and taking in the machinery he prepared himself.

'Ready?' asked Arthur as he watched Fish from above. The Boxtroll gave Arthur a wink and the motor started.

'Here we go!'

*The little submarine started down the canal*

The little submarine started down the canal. Arthur stood with his head out of the conning tower, calling down instructions for steering, and soon they were almost out of sight of Grandfather and the other boxtrolls. Arthur returned their waves until he could see them no more.

'I heard Kipper say that they were going to stop in Bristol tonight so we can catch them up there. Do you think you could work out how to submerge this thing, Fish?'

Fish came to the bottom of the ladder and looked up at Arthur.

'It's just I don't want Willbury to see us. If I can climb on board and hide until they are out to sea, they are not going to turn round just to drop me off, are they?'

Fish smiled and nodded.

*Fish smiled and nodded*

*The ship had tied up on Bristol's main quay for the night*

## Chapter 14

# A Farewell to Harbour

The ship had tied up on Bristol's main quay for the night and the crew had gone ashore for a last drink before the voyage. Willbury had joined them for a sherry and had even asked the doctor to come along for one, but he had refused, saying that he needed to prepare the maps for the voyage.

At daybreak the crew assembled on deck. Tom was still acting as captain and stood at his post on the bridge with a pilot who had come aboard to guide them out of harbour.

'Order of the day?' asked Kipper.

'We are going to use the steam engine until we get out into the channel. Then after we have dropped the pilot off, we'll put up the sails and off we go!'

*Tom at his post with the pilot*

There was a cry from the deck. 'When's breakfast?'

It was the doctor. He was dressed in a huge pink dressing gown and slippers.

'Kipper, will you see to our guest!' ordered Tom.

Kipper took him down to the galley and told him to help himself to porridge and treacle. A few minutes later Kipper returned to find the saucepan gone, along with the large jug of treacle. Later still Kipper found the empty pan and jug on the sideboard in the kitchen.

'Big eater, that doctor. Wouldn't have thought it to look at him.'

*Soon they were out in the channel*

Tom gave the order to cast off. The beam of the engine started to rise and fall and the ship moved slowly out from the harbour wall. Soon they were out in the channel and making their way down towards the sea. The morning tide was with them and they made good progress. After an hour under the guidance of the pilot, they reached the estuary and the pilot was taken off in a small boat.

*The pilot was taken off in a small boat*

As they were now free of the channel and in a fresh breeze, Tom ordered the sails be hoisted. There were happy cries at this as the crew had not been under sail for a long time now and a good wind in sails is something that brings real joy to a sailor.

'Feels great, doesn't it!' Tom called to Kipper.

'Blooming fantastic!'

Shortly the doctor appeared fully dressed.

'When do you think we will reach international waters?' he asked.

Tom was surprised by the question but asked Marjorie, who was acting as navigator.

'I think about three hours.'

'Do you think you could let me know when we are there?' asked the doctor.

'Yes. But why?'

There was no reply. The doctor had disappeared below.

'I wonder what's on his mind?' said Tom.

'Probably worried about it getting rough as the waters get deeper.'

The wind picked up and the ship started to surge forward.

After an hour or so the doctor reappeared and asked if there was a snack he could have.

'After all that porridge?' sputtered Kipper.

'I think it must be the sea air.'

Kipper took him down below again and gave him a large cake tin full of bread pudding.

'That should keep you happy.'

The doctor opened the tin and smiled. 'Well, it should do for the moment. What time is lunch?'

*'What time is lunch?'*

'Have you got hollow legs?'

'Something like that.'

At twelve Marjorie took a reading with the sextant and
started to work out their position. They could just about
still see land, but she wanted to get into practice. While she
was doing the calculations lunch was served, and the doctor
disappeared with another tray full of food.

*At twelve Marjorie took a reading with the sextant*

Marjorie enjoyed the maths for the calculations and took
another reading an hour or so later when land had
disappeared. After some time with a book of tables and a
chart she declared that they were now in international
waters.

'Shall I go down and tell the doctor?' asked Kipper.
'Perhaps he'd like to celebrate with a little snack.'

'I think it would be courteous,' replied Tom.

Kipper headed below, and then returned. 'He says he will
be up in a few minutes . . . with a little surprise for us.'

'Oh goodie. I love surprises,' chirped Tom.

*'I've lined up a little surprise for you all.'*

## Chapter 15

# SURPRISE!

The doctor appeared, made his way to the bridge, and spoke to Tom.

'I've lined up a little surprise for you all.'

'That is very kind of you. There was no need.'

'It would make me very happy if you would indulge me in my little eccentricities.'

'I am sure we can do that,' said Marjorie.

'I would like the surprise to have its full effect. Would you mind ordering everybody on deck and joining them there? Then I want everybody to close their eyes and turn away while I get everything ready.'

This seemed like great fun. Tom asked the doctor to hold the wheel, then he marched to the edge of the bridge.

'All hands on deck . . . for a surprise!' The crew assembled, and Tom, Kipper, and Marjorie joined them.

'The doctor wants to give us all a big surprise. We've to turn our backs and close our eyes.'

They did as they were told.

'Keep your eyes closed and count to a hundred,' the doctor called out.

The crew started to count aloud.

*'No peeping!'*

'No peeping!' added the doctor.

As the counting reached ninety, everybody was just bursting with excitement.

'Ninety-one, ninety-two, ninety-three, ninety-four, ninety-five . . . ' Some of the crew almost passed out with excitement. ' . . . ninety-six, ninety-seven, ninety-eight, ninety-nine, one hundred!'

The crew all spun round to find themselves facing fifteen blunderbusses, five trotting badgers, twenty men in tall hats and grubby suits and, standing at the front of this mob, one particularly unpleasant-looking failed ex-cheese merchant and master criminal with a grin right across his face.

'Surprise!' smirked Archibald Snatcher.

*'Surprise!'*

NOGENS SENTENTIA PRO IGNARUS

1 GROAT

# THE ·Ratbridge·Gazette·

# CHEESE ATTACKED!
## WOMAN CHARGED.

A Mrs Fingle (52) of Innox Rd, Ratbridge, was found asleep this morning on the banks of the River Rat amongst the savaged remains of a CHEESE! Pieces of RIND bearing the evidence of human tooth marks lay strewn about the ground where she lay. Once awoken the

guilty woman denied the crime. Police have locked Mrs Fingle (38) up, and she is to appear before magistrates later today.

We thought the barbaric & medieval practice of consumption of cheese would have been stopped by the outlawing of cheese hunting, but yet again the law is flouted. This paper will campaign for the heaviest of sentences for those who take it upon themselves to prey on these defenceless creatures. Cheese hunting and eating has to be stamped out!*

*detailed engravings of the terrible crime scene and gory reconstructions of her savage acts of bestial cheese eating on pages 2,4,5,7,9.10,11, and 14, and you can read more in a special Cheese Crime edition tomorrow morning.

# DOCTOR SAVES TOWN WITH WONDER CURE!

Hundreds of Ratbridge's townsfolk have been cured of their ills by recently arrived Dr I. Snook, and his wonder drug 'BLACK JOLLOP'. The cure-all dispensed by this modern day saint from his newly

opened Spa and clinic, is, he says, only paying back a debt he says the people of the town are owed.

What has Ratbridge done to deserve such a wondrous thing? The doctor would not say as he dispensed free treatment to all those in need. And there were many of them! In fact so many that the supply of Black Jollop is now exhausted! What is to be done? How are those afflicted by ills to be cured? Must the Doctor's work come to an untimely end?

No, for coming to his aid are the crew of the Ratbridge Nautical Laundry who offered to set sail to fetch supplies of the key ingredient from a source in the southern seas. Amid scenes of jubilation the Laundry cast off from its position in the canal last evening and set sail on its voyage. May the winds speed their passage and fortune guide their path!

**Mangled Marrows or Crushed Chrysanthemums? See inside for full story of mass destruction of town's greenhouses.**

*One gull tried dive-bombing the strange tube*

## Chapter 16

# CATCHING UP

As the sun was setting over Bristol the previous evening, a few seagulls watched a periscope wander between the moored ships. One gull tried dive-bombing the strange tube, but after banging his beak on the metal, gave up and went to look for a meal elsewhere. Below the periscope Arthur and Fish were taking in turns, looking for the *Laundry*.

After a few minutes they spied the ship. Then the periscope made its way to a quiet corner of the dock and disappeared behind the hulk of an old fishing boat.

Soon two figures made their way quietly along the quayside, and up the unattended gangplank of the *Laundry*. Once on deck, Arthur looked for somewhere to hide. By the steps to the forecastle was the large barrel full of apples. Arthur approached it and lifted the lid.

'Quick Fish. Help me throw the apples over the side.'

It took the two stowaways a few minutes to make enough room to hide, but once they had, Arthur helped Fish climb into the barrel, then followed him in, and closed the lid over them. They settled themselves down amongst the last of the apples.

*They settled themselves down amongst the last of the apples*

'I suppose this is what it would be like in a giant squirrel's nest,' Arthur whispered to Fish.

The dim light of the moon and sound of lapping water from the dock made their way through the bunghole in the side of the barrel, and soon they were both asleep. Not even the return of the now rowdy crew awoke them, and it was only the rolling of the boat as it reached open waters that broke their slumbers.

*Arthur knelt up and looked out of the bunghole*

Arthur knelt up and looked out of the bunghole. Outside he could see his friends in the bright light of day. He watched Tom the rat walking past the barrel carrying a small coil of rope. Arthur was about to call out, but stopped when he remembered that they were hiding, and that until he was sure that the ship would not turn back, he'd better not reveal himself. So he made do with watching until he heard some deep rumbling and a belch behind him. He turned to see Fish breakfasting on one of the remaining apples.

'Good idea!' declared Arthur, and he grabbed an apple for himself.

For the next hour or two Fish and Arthur took turns to look out of the bunghole. Everything seemed very ordered and the rats and pirates seemed to be in their element. Arthur caught a glimpse of Willbury from time to time and then he noticed the doctor coming up to the deck from below.

Arthur watched as the doctor made his way up to the stern and spoke with Tom and Marjorie. Then Tom called

out some orders and the whole crew appeared on deck. This blocked out Arthur's view. All he could see were the backs of his friends standing around the barrel.

After some more orders that Arthur couldn't make out, everybody seemed to turn towards the barrel and started counting out loud. What was happening? he wondered. Were they playing a game? The counting reached one hundred and stopped. The crew turned their backs to the barrel again and there was silence apart from a familiar voice. A small gap opened in the crowd in front of the barrel and to Arthur's horror he saw . . .

ARCHIBALD SNATCHER!

*ARCHIBALD SNATCHER!*

*Faces turned from surprise to horror*

## Chapter 17

# SNATCHER RETURNS!

The looks on the crew's faces turned from surprise to horror, and as they did Willbury grabbed Marjorie's arm.

'It's that awful man.'

Snatcher smiled.

'Good day my old friends. It is sooooo nice to see you all again. And how joyous it is to give you all a surprise!'

'What are you doing here?' shouted Kipper.

'Silence you squabs!' hissed Snatcher. He signalled to his men and they cocked their weapons.

'Steady now. We don't want any accidents, do we? Wouldn't want to hurt me crew.'

'What do you mean crew? We ain't your crew!' shouted Kipper.

'That I'm afraid is where you're wrong. I'm the captain now and you will address me as such!'

There was silence.

'Let me explain. The contract you signed with the doctor here gave him total control over this voyage.' He pulled the contract from his pocket and waved it in the air. 'And he decided to appoint me captain.'

*He pulled the contract from his pocket and waved it in the air*

The doctor, who was standing by Snatcher's side, smiled and nodded.

'My first order as captain is to have you lot demoted to "sailors third class"!'

There were gasps from the crew.

'And my second order is that all my friends here is officers.' Snatcher pointed at his evil cronies.

'Now remember, disobeying the captain or any of his officers is severely punishable.' Snatcher and his 'officers' giggled.

'He can't do this, can he?' Tom exclaimed to Willbury. 'He's a convicted criminal and criminals can't be captains. The law says so.'

Snatcher moved closer.

'Which law is that? English law? You might not have noticed but we're more than ten miles from the coast, and that means we are out of English waters and therefore English law don't apply. What does apply is international law. And under that law I'm your captain.'

'Is that true?' asked Kipper.

'Yes, I am afraid so,' replied Willbury.

'Yes indeedy do!' smiled Snatcher. 'My word is law on this ship, and if I have trouble with you lot, you'll be feeling the full extent of . . . the law . . . As sailors I am sure you know disobedience can be seen as mutiny, and the punishment for mutiny is . . . ?'

The crew looked very pale.

'What's the punishment for mutiny?' muttered Marjorie.

Kipper ran his finger across his throat and made a gagging noise.

*Kipper ran his finger across his throat*

'Right! Want to get off on the right footing, don't we?' Snatcher jibed. 'So the crew's quarters are to be cleared for the officers, and "sailors third class" will be in the bilges. Once that's sorted I want a four course lunch, hammocks rigged up here in the sun for me and me officers, all the beer and rum to be stowed in my cabin, the entire ship scrubbed from top to toe . . . And I want a proper captain's hat—one with feathers and a big anchor on it.'

'He's power mad!' whispered Kipper.

Snatcher went on. 'I'd like lunch to be ready by one o'clock and you lot,' he said, smirking, 'will get your grub when I've decided you deserve it.'

The crew didn't move.

'Get to it! I 'eard about that cat-o'-nine-tails. Sounds like something a captain might use.'

The crew were suddenly filled with life and set about Snatcher's list. First the crew cleared their things from the crew deck and carefully lowered them through a hatch into the bilges, while the officers made themselves at home. Then hammocks were strung up. Snatcher's hammock was hung on the stern deck so he could keep an eye on things and give orders from it.

Tom found a captain's hat, decorated it with a few gull feathers and some tin foil, then presented it to the new captain.

'Ain't you got some fluffier feathers?'

'I'm afraid not.'

'Well I suppose this will have to do,' said Snatcher as he lay back in his hammock. 'Now splice the mainbrace or something!'

*'Ain't you got some fluffier feathers?'*

Kipper (who was at the wheel) was not quite sure what to do, but Marjorie helped him out.

'I think the captain means that you set course at full speed south, south-west.'

'Yeah. That's right,' agreed Snatcher. 'And you can bring me a compass. I don't want us going somewhere I'm not expecting.'

Marjorie provided Snatcher with a small pocket compass, then looked at the charts while Kipper set course and called for more sail.

*A small pocket compass*

On the main deck sailor third class Nibble was having problems. The scrubbing played hell with his knees. As he looked about to make sure nobody was watching so he could rest, he suddenly heard his name.

'Pssst . . . Mr Nibble . . . Pssst . . . Willbury . . . '

Willbury looked around and but couldn't see where the voice was coming from.

'I'm over here . . . In the barrel!'

Cautiously Willbury looked over at the barrel and saw an eye staring back at him through the bunghole. Checking that nobody was watching him he moved closer to the barrel and started to pretend to scrub the deck around it.

*He moved closer to the barrel and started to pretend to scrub the deck*

'Who is it?'

'Me! Arthur!'

Willbury stopped what he was doing for a moment.

'Arthur? What are you doing in there?'

'I wanted to come along. So me and Fish followed you and hid in here.'

Nervously Willbury looked about before speaking.

'You've got Fish in there as well?'

'Yes. Right cosy it is too.'

'Well, you had better just stay in there for the moment. Did you see what has just happened?'

'Yes. Snatcher! What can we do about it?'

'I am not sure there is anything we can do. But you stay hidden.'

'OK. Is there any chance you could get us some food? Both of us are rather sick of apples.'

'I will see what I can do.'

Willbury moved away from the barrel and started scrubbing his way towards Tom who was working not far away. Arthur watched as Willbury whispered to Tom.

A smile broke across Tom's face as he looked towards the barrel. Then Willbury and Tom moved around, passing on the news to their friends. In turn each of their friends took a look towards the barrel and smiled.

Over the next hour several 'sailors third class' appeared near the barrel and pushed sausages and other suitable food through the bunghole. At one point Bert appeared with a bucket and a funnel. When no one was looking Bert put the funnel through the hole and Fish and Arthur took turns to drink the water he poured through. They had been very thirsty and the water was extremely welcome, but not long after, the need to relieve themselves became overpowering. The next time Willbury came by Arthur explained the situation.

*Fish and Arthur took turns to drink*

'I think while lunch is being served we might be able to cause enough of a distraction to get you out for a minute.'

'Please, please do!' implored Arthur.

Lunch was delivered to Snatcher and his men, in the form of a buffet. After some words with Willbury, Tom had arranged for it to be laid out on the forecastle. Snatcher and most of his men took full advantage of it, leaving just a few officers with blunderbusses watching the main deck.

Then Arthur's friends made great play of bringing up some trays of snacks for the guards and while they were distracted, Marjorie and Bert slipped the top off the barrel and helped their friends climb out. Arthur and Fish quickly relieved themselves over the side of the ship and were helped back into the barrel.

As the lid was put back in place, Marjorie smiled at
Arthur.

'Glad to have you both on board. I think we might be
needing your help.'

*'I think we might be needing your help.'*

NOGENS SENTENTIA PRO IGNARUS

1 GROAT

# THE ·Ratbridge·Gazette·

# LOCAL CHEESES IN PERIL!

Late last night a frightful new attack was made on the cheeses that live just outside the town. Night-watchman Mr Ebenezer Paint (63) heard hysterical bleating at about two a.m. as he performed his duties.

'I was just brewing up a cuppa on the town wall when I heard a right pitiful noise. So I had a quick look and was shocked. There was a crowd of maniacs chasing some poor cheeses across the fields.'

Mr Paint (97) told of the horrific scenes of carnage as the mob caught up with the cheeses. 'It was horrid. I never want to see anything like that ever again! They descended on 'em like beasts. Terrible it were!'

'When it was over the mob came back towards the town, and after seeing what they did to them cheeses I hid meself.'

Later Mr Paint (14) summoned the police and led them to the crime scene.

'It were not a sight for those with a weak disposition,' reported a police spokesperson.

After cordoning off the crime scene a search was made for the offenders, but none were apprehended.

This paper is outraged that such a thing could happen twice within a week. We have to stop it! To this end we are now going to offer a reward of twenty-five groats for information leading to a conviction of these criminals (terms and conditions apply).

*Marjorie took out all the maps*

## Chapter 18

# SAIL AND STEAM

After lunch the doctor gave Marjorie a small piece of paper with a map reading on it.

'This is where we're heading.'

Marjorie took out all the maps that were kept in a locker by the wheel, and after spending quite a lot of time studying them she spoke.

'Are you sure this is right? This reading gives the position of a small island in the Pacific!'

'Is that a problem for you?' Snatcher snapped.

'It's halfway round the world!'

'And your point is?'

Marjorie looked up at Kipper and shook her head. 'It's a long, long way. Have you ever sailed that far?'

Kipper shook his head.

'Well, you better get to it then,' smiled Snatcher.

'It could take months. I doubt we have enough provisions for a journey like that.'

'Well, you better work out how we can get there fast then. One thing you can bet on is it ain't going to be me and me officers who go short.'

Marjorie gave Kipper a worried look.

'Do you mind if I call a meeting? I'll have to organize things if we're to speed this journey up.'

'All right, but I will be keeping a very close eye on yer. Don't want no funny business.'

Marjorie called the crew on deck.

'Our captain is asking us to sail to the Southern Pacific.'

This was met by silence.

'If we're to make it before the food runs out we're going to have to use steam. I want half the crew to work the sails and the other half stoking the boiler.'

'Hang on a minute,' snapped Snatcher from his hammock. 'Leave us a cook. I want me grub.'

*'Hang on a minute.'*

'Very well. So apart from the cook I want you divided in two. We'll work shifts and get going as fast as we can.'

Two teams formed and soon the boiler was back in action. Once the steam was up the ship started surging forward and Marjorie took several readings over the course of the next few hours. Using these calculations she tried to work out if they would make it before running out of food and fuel.

'I reckon it's going to be a very tight thing,' she muttered to Kipper. 'If we have any hold ups we're done for, and the last part of the journey will have to be under sail as we'll have run out of fuel by then.'

'Can't we stop somewhere and get some more?' asked Kipper.

'I can't see Snatcher wanting us to stop off. Might give us a chance to escape.'

'If we are going to the South Pacific, does that mean we have to go around the Cape?'

'Yes . . . yes it does.'

Kipper looked worried.

'Not sure the ship will stand up to that.'

'It will have to.'

The ship forged ahead. Even though all the crew were now very worried by the voyage, they could not help but somewhat enjoy the feeling of the ship travelling at high speed. Snatcher loved the speed and soon went to the forecastle to watch the waves crash on the bows.

Kipper turned to Marjorie.

*The ship forged ahead*

'The ship is going well.'

'Yes. We might even make it.'

'Do you think that's a good thing?'

'Why?'

'Have you asked yourself why Snatcher would want to go somewhere to collect something to make medicine to give away?'

'No . . . I wonder what he is up to?'

'So do I.'

'You can bet we don't know the full story.'

'Yes, but I just can't work it out.'

For the rest of the day Snatcher wandered about giving pointless orders, and finally asked for supper. He seemed so happy with the way things were going that he offered the crew food.

'I think even the sailors third class might deserve a crumb. When me and me officers have finished and the washing up is done I think I might allow them a light supper. Let them break open the hardtack.'

'What's hardtack?' asked one of the officers.

'It's ship's biscuits.'

'Sounds nice.'

Kipper, who was still at the wheel, didn't look happy at the prospect.

'More like lumps of rock with worms in. We only keep them for emergencies on long voyages. They are so hard you have to soak them just to be able to scrape off a layer with your teeth.'

'But I understand they really are very nutritious,' giggled Snatcher.

*'More like lumps of rock with worms in'*

As the sun went down supper was served for Snatcher and his men and after it an order was given to move all food apart from the hardtack to the captain's cabin. The crew were unhappy but with blunderbusses being waved around, the stores were soon stowed in Snatcher's quarters.

Then a large wooden crate of biscuits was brought up on deck.

'Here's your rations. I am giving you the lot. If you run out then it's your bad luck so I suggest you keep some back.'

*A little more edible…*

The crew took some biscuits and used mugs of lukewarm water to soak them in to try to make them a little more edible. After just about getting them down, those who were on the overnight watch settled to their tasks while the rest of the crew were locked in the bilges and tried to get some sleep. This was difficult as there was water slopping about and the soap that was left over from when the bilges had been used for laundry now created mountains of frothy damp foam.

'At least it is clean,' muttered Willbury.

*'At least it is clean'*

On the night watch Tom was in charge of the wheel. Between taking their position from the stars and steering he kept a watchful eye on the barrel. Around midnight the officers had cocoa and wandered up to the forecastle leaving Tom alone. Quickly he tied the wheel in position and crept down on deck to the barrel.

'Arthur!' he whispered. 'It's safe. The guards aren't looking. If you need to get out and . . . you know what . . . '

The top of the barrel lifted and out popped Arthur and Fish's heads.

*Out popped Arthur's and Fish's heads*

'It's good to get some fresh air,' whispered Arthur.

Tom pointed up to the forecastle with one hand and put a finger to his lips with the other. Arthur and Fish climbed out of the barrel, and had a quick stretch in the shadows before Tom signalled to them to follow him to the store cabin under the forecastle. Once inside he spoke.

'This is blooming awful. Snatcher has taken control of the food and there doesn't seem to be much we can do about it.'

'Do you know what Snatcher is up to?' asked Arthur.

'No. We've all been trying to work it out. Got to be something dodgy. Snatcher never does anything for anyone unless there is a lot in it for Snatcher.'

'I hope we find out before it is too late.'

Footsteps creaked on the boards of the deck above them and Tom signalled them back to the barrel.

'I've got a little something for you to make life more comfortable.' Tom handed Arthur something small wrapped in a hanky, before closing the lid over his friends.

*Tom handed Arthur something small wrapped in a hanky*

*'Captain . . .'*

## Chapter 19

# PARTY PLAN

For the next few days the ship sped towards the South
Atlantic. With the combination of steam and sail it was only
going to be a few days before they reached the Equator.

Bert had an idea. Without telling the others he
approached Snatcher.

'Captain . . . '

'Yes?'

'Did you know that it is traditional to have a party when
you cross the Equator?'

Snatcher looked very doubtful. 'Why would I want to
hold a party for scum?'

'It wouldn't be for us, sir. No, it's just to honour the
captain and for a bit of fun.'

Snatcher was intrigued. 'Is it indeed? Tell me more.'

'Well it involves you and an assistant dressing up. You as

Neptune, the king of the sea, and your assistant as a mermaid.'

'A mermaid!' Snatcher looked surprised. 'And then what?'

'Well, everybody has to come on deck and you have to punish any officer who has never been across the Equator for any crimes they might have committed.'

*Neptune with assistant mermaid*

'This is starting to sound fun. And how do I punish these miscreants?'

'Nothing too nasty. Usually a large tub of goo is made up from anything we can find around the ship. You have a big brush and splat it on them!'

A smile spread over Snatcher's face. The idea appealed.

'This sounds like a tradition I might like to carry on,' said Snatcher, mulling it over. 'But I do think it's pretty cheeky of you to come here and ask me to splat my own men . . .'

Bert looked a little worried—until Snatcher gave him a

wink. 'But this is too good an opportunity to miss out on. So when do we get to the equator?'

'Late tomorrow at this rate.'

There were several officers sitting with Snatcher, and they were now looking daggers at Bert.

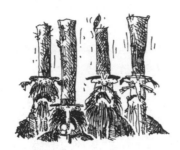

*They were now looking daggers at Bert*

'If it is to be done properly, you'll arrive on deck as Neptune about ten minutes before we cross the Equator—with your mermaid assistant.'

'And let me guess . . . You lot get to watch me goo my officers?'

Bert tried not to look happy at this.

'Very well, I shall do it,' said Snatcher. 'You're in charge of getting the goo and costumes ready.'

'Yes, captain!' said Bert, saluting. 'And who'll be the mermaid? I'll need to know so the costume fits.'

Snatcher thought for a minute. 'I think my friend the doctor would do.'

The doctor, who'd been listening, started to protest.

'No, please not me.'

'It is either that or being punished for disobeying orders!'

'What's the goo made of?'

'Given what we have to hand I think bilge water, treacle, old oil, glue . . . That sort of stuff.'

The officers looked outraged and more than somewhat worried.

'All right. A merman I shall be.'

'Mermaid,' Snatcher corrected him.

'Very well. A mermaid.'

'By the way, what does this Neptune bloke wear?' asked Snatcher.

'A crown of shells and a cloak. Sort of fishy theme. It'll be very elegant.'

'Well just you make sure it's not too fishy, or I'll be doing some punishing of whoever's responsible.'

'Would my costume be very fishy?' asked the doctor.

'Mermaids is fish!' answered Snatcher. 'So I think fishy is the very soul of your costume.'

Bert snapped a salute. 'I shall get right to it then, captain!'

*'I shall get right to it then, captain!'*

NOGENS SENTENTIA PRO IGNARUS

1 GROAT

# THE ·Ratbridge· Gazette·

# RECOVERED TENNIS ELBOW SUFFERER FOUND IN POSSESSION OF CHEESY MORSELS!

At daybreak today one of our reporters accompanied the local constabulary in the raid that apprehended a suspected member of the mob that has been carrying out the recent cheese outrages. At 6.47 a.m. police raided the dwellings of Mrs J. Topperthwaite after a tip-off, and there discovered cheesy morsels hidden in a sofa.

The anonymous information was supplied by Ms Maya Singer (a cleaning lady), who suspected her employer of 'cheese eating' after finding scatterings of fermented lactose while cleaning Mrs Topperthwaite's drawing room.

'I couldn't believe it! She seemed such a nice old dear, but once I found the crumbs of cheese I knew it were my duty to report her. Do I get the reward now?'

Mrs Topperthwaite is now in custody. After her foul feast of cheese we hope she gets dished up her 'just desserts'!

*It did actually look quite good*

## Chapter 20

# A BARREL OF FUN?

In spare moments from their other duties the 'sailors third class' set about work on the costumes and goo. Snatcher gave them permission to search the ship (apart from his cabin) for anything they needed, and the crew took full advantage. Although officers were sent to watch the search, they were careful not to cause any problems in case it made Snatcher unhappy. The officers were already worried about any crimes they might have committed that Snatcher might use against them.

The next day around teatime Bert delivered the costumes and told Snatcher that they would be crossing the Equator at about 8.30 p.m.

'I see you have been hard at work,' Snatcher said as he admired his Neptune outfit, then he put it on. It did actually look quite good. The crown of shells looked rather regal in a shabby sort of way.

Snatcher turned his attention to the mermaid costume. 'My darling doctor, you're going to look like the most beautiful . . . fish.'

Then, eyeing up the costume, Snatcher asked, 'Do mermaids have legs?'

*'Do mermaids have legs?'*

'Not really,' said Bert. 'Just a tail. But we gave the costume legs so that the doctor would be able to walk.'

'Stitch the legs together!' ordered Snatcher.

Bert set off with the costume under his arm and a smile on his face. He soon returned with the costume altered as Snatcher had asked. Snatcher took a good look and then spoke.

'Good! Doctor, would you like to go and change? I can't wait to see how my Mer-assistant is going to look.'

'Very good . . . ' the doctor mumbled as he went off holding the costume.

'Now, how is the goo?'

'Would you like to come and inspect it, captain?'

'Yes please. I don't want any sub-standard goo.'

Bert led Snatcher to the main deck where a large half-barrel stood, covered by a sheet. Bert whipped the sheet off and Snatcher pulled back as the smell hit him.

'What's in it?'

'Lots of things,' said Bert.

'Not too lethal, I hope.'

'I don't think there is anything in there that would kill anyone,' said Bert.

*Bert whipped the sheet off*

'Smells a bit?'

'Is a bit not enough?'

Snatcher smiled. 'Is it possible to make it smellier?'

'Certainly!'

'Well, get to it then!'

Bert thought for a moment, then grinned.

'Bert? What are you going to use?' asked Tom.

Bert had a twinkle in his eye. 'Wait and see!'

With that he set off across the deck to where the trotting badgers that Snatcher had brought along were being kept in a large crate.

'What do trotting badgers produce that is very, very smelly?' called Bert as he stood by the crate.

'You can't be serious?' said Tom.

'Get me a metal spade,' giggled Bert as he pulled something from his pocket.

'What you got there?' asked Tom.

'Hardtack!'

He waved the biscuit in the air. Suddenly the trotting badgers' noses pricked up and they ran to the barred front of their shelter. Tom handed Bert a spade while the officer looked on in horror.

'Watch this.'

Bert threw the hardtack into the back of the crate and the badgers descended upon it. Quick as a flash Bert then slipped the spade under the bars and scooped up something from the floor, then withdrew the spade.

*Bert slipped the spade under the bars*

Then Bert walked back to the tub of goo and tipped whatever was on the spade into the goo.

'DISGUSTING!' moaned the crew.

There was silence from the officers.

*The goo tub*

*Then Neptune appeared*

Chapter 21

# The King and Queen of the Oceans

At eight-twenty Marjorie took a reading on the sextant and declared they were about to reach the Equator. The ship's bell was rung and the officers reluctantly assembled on deck, while the crew arranged themselves on the forecastle to get a good view. Then Neptune appeared.

Arthur, who had been keeping tabs on things from inside the barrel, was quite impressed with the way Snatcher looked.

'Here, have a look, Fish. This isn't something you'll see every day.' And he moved around the barrel so his friend could view what was happening.

The officers stared at their leader.

Then there was a lot of clonking and swearing and a

mermaid flopped out of the doorway from the stairs and fell flat on the deck. The poor doctor was wearing the tail, a pair of coconuts as a bikini top, and a long wig made from seaweed. He was not happy as he tried to stand up, and moved like a beached seal. Snatcher on the other hand seemed jollier than the crew had ever seen him before. He walked up to the goo tub and raised an old broom he'd been clutching.

*A mermaid flopped out of the doorway from*
*the stairs and fell flat on the deck*

'Bow before the King of the Sea,' he ordered. Everyone did as they were told.

'I am Neptune, King of the Seven Seas, and I have risen from my kingdom to dish out punishment to those who deserve it!'

The 'sailors third class' smiled and the officers started shaking nervously. Snatcher then took out a list from under his cloak and began to read.

'I have decided that each punishment shall fit each crime.' Snatcher scanned the officers to find his first victim before turning his eyes back to the list.

'Gristle! You are guilty of the crime of darning my socks with wire. This is unforgivable and has played havoc with my bunions. Therefore I call you to stand before me, and remove your footwear!'

Gristle came forward. He looked a little puzzled, but took off his shoes and socks.

'Right then. Do your worst!' Gristle said with something approaching defiance.

'Oh I will Gristle. I will!' And Snatcher dipped the broom into the barrel.

The broom broke a thin crust on top of the goo. As the smell hit Gristle he almost fell over. Something chemically horrid had happened to the brew.

'Please . . . no!' said Gristle, backing off.

'If you run away, you'll only make it worse for yourself. I shall be forced to give you a double ration!' warned Snatcher.

Gristle froze.

'I anoint you in the name of Neptune!' intoned Snatcher and he took the goo-laden broom and slowly slopped it onto Gristle's feet. The goo settled like thick treacle on a pudding.

'It terrible, but I can't believe how satisfying it was to watch the appalling man get daubed,' Willbury muttered to Marjorie.

'You are now anointed,' Snatcher proclaimed with a satisfied grin. 'Next please!'

Gristle unstuck himself from the deck, and glooped his way back to his place amongst the officers, but found that a large space cleared around him.

Snatcher handed the list to his mermaid.

The mermaid studied the list and looked a little puzzled.

*Gristle unstuck himself from the deck*

'It says here "Ernest Grunge found guilty of F.O.B."?'

'Yes!' replied Snatcher. 'Fingers on bacon. I noticed his thieving hands disappearing with a rasher I was after at breakfast.'

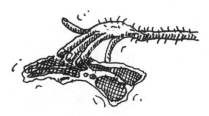

*Fingers on bacon*

A space now cleared around the unfortunate Ernest Grunge. 'I didn't know you wanted that bacon!'

'You is bleedin' common. Didn't your mother tell you to ask before grabbin' the last rasher?'

Grunge shook his head.

'So you need an education then. Roll back your sleeves!' ordered Snatcher.

Grunge crept forward, rolling back his shirtsleeves.

'Hold them out!'

Grunge did as he was told. Snatcher dipped the broom in the goo, and slapped it on the outstretched hands.

'Yuck!' whispered Bert with rather more glee than might be considered polite.

'Grunge, you are now anointed. Who's next?'

'Let's see . . . "Lardwell Fruitfly. N.I.B."'

'Ah yes! My dear Lardwell, I saw you sneaking a look at some of my papers.'

Poor Lardwell Fruitfly looked perplexed. 'I'm sorry, Guv! I was only tidying things up.'

'Well, that is not how it looked to me,' snapped Snatcher.

'Errrr . . . what does N.I.B. stand for?'

'Nose in business! Can you guess what is going to happen next?'

Lardwell looked horrified and started to back away.

'Grab him!'

Two officers grabbed him and pushed him forward.

There was a swish, then a splat, and Lardwell's prominent nose was hidden under a thick coating of goo. As the fumes hit him he fainted.

*There was a swish, then a splat, and Lardwell's prominent nose was hidden under a thick coating of goo*

'Next!' called Snatcher.

Neptune's mermaid was starting to enjoy this, and read off the next entry.

'"Fingle. T.I.J."'

'Ooo! Fingle. You bad lad! Can you guess what T.I.J. stands for?'

'No, but I promise I'll not do it again if you let me off.'

'That may be so but I still think you would benefit from the lesson. So . . . T.I.J?'

Fingle just slowly shook his head.

'Tongue in jam!'

Fingle went white. 'You are not going to put that stuff on my tongue are you?'

'Fingle, you know the punishment has to fit the crime.'
Fingle made a bolt for the mast.
'Get him!' shouted Snatcher.
Fingle managed to reach the mast and shin up the first
nine feet before the officers reached its base.

*Fingle managed to reach the mast*

'OK. Leave him,' snorted Snatcher. 'He'll have to come
down . . . and when he does . . . Mermaid, next on the list,
please.'

Snatcher worked his way down the list and all the officers
apart from Fingle got their just comeuppance. Then
Neptune retired happily to the captain's cabin for a
nightcap and the crew were given the job of hosing down the
punished. There was a pump used to clean out the bilges and
this was easily adapted for the purpose. Kipper took charge.

'Right then. All of you who want a wash, hold on to the
mast with your dirty bits pointed outwards.'

The officers braced themselves and Kipper had the best fifteen minutes of fun of his life, while the crew cheered and watched with glee. By the time the officers were clean, most had very few clothes remaining and those clothes that did remain were in tatters.

*Kipper had the best fifteen minutes of fun of his life*

'Shall I wash out the tub?' Kipper asked.

'I think it is Snatcher's idea that we keep that back for Fingle. Just nail down a lid on it to keep the smell down,' Tom suggested.

A lid was made and it was decided to throw the broom over the side. A few hours later dead fish could be found floating in the wake of the ship.

*A few hours later dead fish could be found floating in the wake of the ship*

**1 GROAT**

# THE ·Ratbridge·Gazette·

# CHEESE SURVIVAL THREATENED IN FURTHER ATTACKS

'After the recent appalling attacks there has been a noticeable decline in cheese numbers. If there are any more losses, our cheeses may not have a large enough breeding population to survive and they could become extinct!' reported Cuthbert Milk, chairman of the Ratbridge Wildlife Conservation Association.

This shocking revelation comes in the shadow of yet another outrage. Only last night police tried to arrest 'Cheesy Crims' returning to the town after another dastardly attack. Unfortunately the police were overpowered and the mob escaped.

These outrages must stop. This paper will
now raise the reward for the capture of
'Cheesy Crims' to 100 groats.

*Arthur put a leg over the edge of the barrel and lifted himself out*

## Chapter 22

# THE NIGHT WATCH

Arthur and Fish had taken it in turns to enjoy the entertainment, and now things had quietened down Arthur's mind had turned to food. That morning they had finally run out of apples and the ship's biscuits that Tom had sneaked in to them were horrid.

'We have to get something else to eat.'

Outside, the crew on the night watch were busy and Arthur was unable to catch anyone's attention.

'Right Fish. I think we are on our own.' After a quick look out of the bunghole Arthur lifted the lid and looked about. With ripped and sodden clothes, the officers who were supposed to be on guard were huddled by the boiler trying to keep warm.

Arthur put a leg over the edge of the barrel and lifted himself out. Fish followed.

'If we make our way round to the other side of the deck we can get down the stairs and might be able to find something,' Arthur whispered.

They crept across the deck and made their way towards the steps leading to the deck below. As they reached the top of the steps, there was a sudden shout from somewhere above.

'Oi, down there. Someone is creeping about!' It was Fingle. He was still up the mast for fear of what might happen if he came down.

*'Oi, down there. Someone is creeping about!'*

The guards looked up but couldn't see Arthur and Fish as the beam engine was in the way.

'Where are they?'

'By the steps to the cabins.'

Arthur and Fish had stopped in their tracks.

'Quick, Fish. Back to the barrel.'

The officers jumped up and drew their blunderbusses.
'FIND THEM!'

A couple of officers ran to the top of the stairway and then turned back to catch the sight of Arthur and Fish running away. A few of the crew members on deck started moving to block the officers' way, but in an instant guns were trained on them and they were ordered not to move.

Arthur reached the front end of the deck and could see there was nowhere to go apart from the forecastle. He and Fish ran up the steps. At the top he turned. The first of the guards was approaching the steps behind them so he took a loose pulley block and threw it.

'Youch!'

*'Youch!'*

The officer stopped as the block bounced off his head. Then he made for the steps again. Arthur threw another block. Again it found its target and the officer pulled back.

'Get the crew below, then I need you all over here to help me deal with this boy and his friend.'

The other officer did as he was told and, with the aid of his blunderbuss, marched the crew below and locked them in the bilges. Then he returned with reinforcements. Arthur could see that the net was closing in on him.

'What are we going to do?' he nervously asked Fish.

Fish gave no answer so Arthur picked up another pulley block, and Fish followed his lead. Seeing them making ready to throw, the officers ran and hid behind the trotting badger crate.

'You put those down, or we'll fire!' came a shout from behind the crate.

Arthur and Fish looked at each other, then turned and threw the blocks as hard as they could in the direction of the shout, then dropped to the ground.

There was a loud crash, an outbreak of snarling from the trotting badgers, and a return of fire. After a few shots the firing stopped as the officers reloaded.

Arthur and Fish stood again, took careful aim and threw two more blocks in the direction of the crate before diving for cover.

Again there was crashing from the direction of the crate, but this time it was followed by screams.

'Must have hit them!' smiled Arthur.

They waited for a few seconds for more gunfire but the screams grew louder and shots didn't come.

Arthur inched his way to the edge of the forecastle and looked over.

The blocks that Arthur and Fish had thrown had done their work but not in the way he had expected. The crate was shattered and the officers were now fending off an attack from the vicious creatures. All the noise and excitement had wound the badgers to a new level of anger, and they were expressing this anger with their jaws

*A new level of anger*

The officers fought to escape and slowly managed to reach the door to the stairwell. The effect of them all trying to get through the door at the same time was a blockage.

The badgers saw their chance and pounced. Teeth sank again and again into flesh and tattered trouser. At the front of the blockage in the stairwell one man manage to loosen himself, and pulled free. This had a dramatic effect. Like a cork the blockage popped out and Snatcher's men tumbled down the stairs. The badgers stopped for a moment in surprise, then followed.

*Then the badgers saw their chance and pounced*

The screaming heap now filled the corridor outside the Captain's cabin.

'Let us in,' screamed one of the officers.

The door opened, and Snatcher was knocked to the ground by the officers, who then scrambled over him. As he sat up he saw the maddened trotting badgers careering along the corridor towards him. With a swift kick of the foot he slammed the door and pushed both of his feet against it. Then a great thump made the door shudder.

'Fetch the desk, blast you!' Snatcher screamed at his men.

Somewhere above, Arthur smiled at Fish.

'I think we'd better block off the top of the stairwell or those badgers will be able to get us.'

They rushed down and across the deck and threw shut the very heavy storm doors that closed off the stairwell. Then Arthur flipped the large iron latch across.

'That's it! We trap the badgers, and the badgers trap Snatcher and his mob! Now what do we do?'

Fish gave a happy gurgle.

'Go and free the others?'

Fish nodded, and they made their way across the deck and down through the forward hatch to the crew deck.

At the end of the crew deck towards the stern was a doorway to the corridor where the badgers were trapped. Fortunately it was closed. Arthur tiptoed towards it, listening to the awful sounds coming from the other side, then turned the key in the lock.

Then they opened the hatch to the bilges.

'Anybody want to go for a walk?'

The eyes of their friends stared up at them.

'Arthur. What has happened?'

*'Anybody want to go for a walk?'*

'Fish and I have sorted everything out. We've taken over the ship and locked Snatcher and his mob in the captain's cabin. I hope you don't mind.'

After a few seconds of stunned silence came a huge joyful shout.

'HOORAY!'

'Come on. I think it's time for us to have our own Equator party.'

It didn't take long for the crew to make their way on deck and start celebrating their freedom.

'I don't know how you did it, but I'm glad you're here.' Arthur turned to see Willbury smiling at him and looking a little embarrassed.

'But you . . .'

'I was only thinking of your best interests.'

*These now shook from the impact of the trotting badgers*

While the crew partied on deck, below, Snatcher and his men had managed to stack the desk and several large sea chests against the door. These now shook from the impact of the trotting badgers.

Snatcher looked about. 'This could have gone better.'

'Pity we don't have any Black Jollop to fix the wounds,' said the doctor.

'Yes. But even I wouldn't poison my men with that stuff.'

*Breakfast had been hardtack and a few small fish*

## Chapter 23

# FREEDOM

'What are we going to do about Snatcher and his mob?' asked Tom the following morning. 'And are we just going to turn around and go home now?'

'And what about food?' added Kipper. Breakfast had been hardtack and a few small fish that the crew had managed to catch over the side.

'I think we might be able to do some negotiation on the food front,' replied Marjorie. 'They're going to be stuck in that cabin until we help them out so I think we hold most of the cards.'

'Yes, I wonder what they'll be prepared to pay for removal of the trotting badgers?' giggled Kipper.

'I don't think totally removing the trotting badgers is our best bet,' smirked Bert. 'I think that just removal of the immediate threat of a good chewing is enough to get us what we want.'

'Sounds like a good idea. Follow me!' Marjorie led the crew up on to the bridge and leant over the stern.

With a boathook she knocked on the window of the captain's cabin, and after a few seconds the window opened and Snatcher's head popped out.

*She knocked on the window of the captain's cabin*

'Good morning!' smiled Marjorie.

'Get us out of here!' Snatcher yelled. 'That is an order.'

'Pardon me,' said Marjorie. 'What did you say?'

'I said get us out of here. AND THAT IS AN ORDER!' repeated Snatcher. 'If you don't I shall have you all for mutiny!'

'I am very sorry,' apologized Marjorie. 'But I am afraid we can't hear you.'

The crew all laughed.

'Will you *please* get us out of here,' Snatcher asked, a little more politely.

'I don't think we can,' said Bert. 'The trotting badgers might attack us if we tried. And you wouldn't want any of your crew injured, would you?'

'I just might . . . ' muttered Snatcher under his breath. Then he spoke louder. 'So what are you expecting us to do? Stay in here for the rest of the trip?'

'I should say that is a distinct possibility,' said Marjorie.

'Can't you lower a rope ladder and let us climb out? Please?'

'That might also be dangerous. We wouldn't want any of you falling in the sea,' said Marjorie. 'I think it best for everybody if you stay where you are.'

'Blow you! Are you just going to leave us here? Those trotting badgers could break through any time.'

*'Those trotting badgers could break through any time'*

'Well I think things can be organized properly to stop that happening,' replied Marjorie.

'How do you mean?' snapped Snatcher.

'Well, it would be very inconvenient for the captain to be stuck in the cabin during the rest of the trip. It might be better for him to be on deck with his crew.'

'I couldn't agree with you more!' said Snatcher, looking a little happier.

'Well, as you agree, and are stuck down there, I suggest you appoint a new captain.'

'Blowed if I will!' Snatcher was furious at the suggestion.

'Well, without the correct orders the crew might not be able to help protect you from those vicious badgers,' Marjorie said with a smile.

'I will not be pushed around by a . . . WOMAN! Get me out of here at once!'

'I am sorry. I didn't hear you.' Then Marjorie turned to the rest of the crew who were watching. 'Did any of you hear anything?'

The crew all shook their heads, and laughed.

Arthur smiled and waved to his friends to come close. 'I have an idea that might help.'

'What would that be?' asked Willbury.

'It's a little bit naughty, but I think it'll help Snatcher come round to our way of thinking.'

'Well in the circumstances, anything "a little bit naughty" might be all right. What is it?'

'Watch!' said Arthur. Then he crossed the stern deck and went down the steps to the locked doorway.

The crew watched as Arthur raised his fists and started banging them on the doors.

'WAKEY, WAKEY, badgers! WAKEY, WAKEY!'

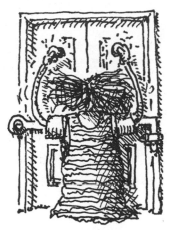

*'WAKEY, WAKEY, badgers!'*

This seemed to do the trick. There was a flurry of snarling and banging from below deck, followed by screams of fear from the captain's cabin.

The crew rushed back to the stern rail to see what would happen.

Snatcher's head popped out of the cabin window and he started yelling.

'Quick! They're breaking through!'

'It will cost you.'

'What?'

There was some more banging and screaming from below and Snatcher looked nervously back into the cabin.

'What do you want?'

'Half the food.'

'Never!'

'Half the food!'

'NO!'

'Well then, enjoy yourselves with your furry little friends,' Kipper called down.

Snatcher looked panicked. 'OK, OK! But what do I get in return?'

'How about some metal sheeting, a hammer, and nails?'

'Perfect! Lower it down quick and I'll send up the food.'

'I think we both know who's to be trusted around here,' said Marjorie. 'You send up the food, and then we'll send down the metal sheet and tools.'

'OK! OK! Just send down a rope.'

Marjorie leant over and whispered in Kipper's ear. 'Tell Arthur to bang on the door some more.'

Marjorie spoke again as Kipper disappeared. 'We need to sort out this captain thing.'

Snatcher was about to reply when the noise of badgers and screams started up again.

'Would you like to appoint my friend Tom as captain so he can get the rope organized?'

A nervous Snatcher nodded.

'All right, I appoint that rat Tom captain.

A rope was lowered with a large net on the end and very quickly the food was loaded. Then, as promised, a sheet of tin, some nails, and a hammer were sent down in exchange. While Snatcher and his mob nailed the metal up, the crew had their first good meal in days.

As they ate they discussed what to do next. No one was quite sure; but soon they would have their minds made up for them.

*Then, as promised, a sheet of tin, some nails, and a hammer were sent down in exchange*

NOGENS SENTENTIA PRO IGNARUS

1 GROAT

# ·Ratbridge·Gazette·

# POLICE BRING IN HOUNDS TO CATCH CHEESY CRIMS

In an attempt to track down the perpetrators of the ongoing cheese outrages, a number of cheese-hounds have been purchased from the Ratbridge Holiday Home for Cats and Dogs, and Economy Pie Company. The hounds are being used because they have a keen sense of smell and a strong desire for

cheese. Already the dogs have helped to close the net on the Cheesy Crims. Yesterday afternoon seventeen people were arrested after the hounds tracked the scent to various addresses in the town.

In one surprising raid, the Honourable Mr Clifford Swage (Mayor of Ratbridge) was detained. This paper says 'Let justice be done. No one is above the law!'

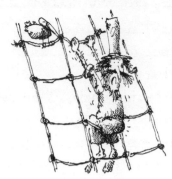

*He was cold, hungry, and his bottom had a painful groove in it*

## Chapter 24

# THE BIG SECRET

Fingle had had enough of watching life from up in the rigging. He was cold, hungry, and his bottom had a painful groove in it where he'd been sitting on a rope. Giving himself up to the crew couldn't be much worse. So he climbed down and presented himself to Bert and a couple of the larger pirates.

'What shall we do with this sneak? He's the one that almost got Arthur caught. Shall I rough him up?' Bert was straining at the leash.

'We'll have none of that.' Willbury had appeared with Arthur by his side. 'I think he might answer a few questions though.'

'What do you want to know?' asked the dishevelled Fingle.

'Some information about Black Jollop, this trip, and what Snatcher is up to with the doctor.'

'I ain't telling you nothin'.'

'When did you last eat?'

'Days ago . . . ' said Fingle, as he held his shrunken stomach.

'Bert, could you bring me a fresh bacon sandwich?'

'Is that for me?' asked the hopeful Fingle.

'It might be, but then again I might fancy it, or perhaps Bert would.'

'Yup! I fancy a bacon sandwich all right. A nice thick one with loads of ketchup and butter.'

There was an odd empty gurgling sound from Fingle's stomach.

Bert smiled slyly at hearing the noise. 'As I remember there is only enough bacon left for one really good sandwich. I do feel quite peckish, but bacon makes such good fishing bait. Maybe we should just throw it over the side instead?'

'Stop it! This is cruel and unusual punishment, this is! Blooming torture!'

'To you it may be torture, but to me it is just a sandwich. I can take it or leave it. Actually I don't know if I fancy one really, maybe I'll just throw it over the side.'

*'Stop it! This is cruel and unusual punishment, this is!'*

'You're mad, and cruel!' Fingle looked very worried. 'What do you want to know?'

The retired lawyer stood and took hold of his lapels.

'I want to know about the Black Jollop. Are the effects permanent?'

'As far as I know,' stuttered Fingle.

'And why would Archibald Snatcher be behind a scheme to hand out free medicine to the people of Ratbridge?'

Fingle started to twitch nervously. 'It's more than my life's worth to tell yer.'

The sandwich arrived and Fingle's eyes fell upon it.

Willbury took the sandwich and sniffed it. 'Very nice. Finest Gloucester Old Spot, I think?'

*'Finest Gloucester Old Spot, I think?'*

'Correct, Mr Nibble. The bread is just out of the oven, and I think they've used un-salted Danish butter,' Bert added.

The saliva was starting to run down Fingle's chin.

'You can't do this to me. I, I, I . . . If I tells yer, yer promise me yer won't put me back with Snatcher?'

'If you don't tell me what I want to know I will put you back with him. And I might just thank you in front of him for telling me about the Black Jollop even if you haven't.'

Fingle went white.

'Whereas if you tell me everything I just might let you have a couple of rounds of fat juicy bacon sandwiches.'

'What do you want to know?'

'So, the Black Jollop?'

'It's poison.'

Everybody but Fingle looked shocked. 'Can I have a bite now?'

'No, not yet. What on earth do you mean "it's poison"? We've all seen it cure people!'

'Well, it does cure things. Loads of things. But there's a downside.'

'What downside?' snapped Willbury.

'It has effects. Right interesting ones. And I ain't telling you more until I get a bite.'

'Very well.' Willbury held out the sandwich and two large pirates holding Fingle let him lean forward to take a bite.

'Tell me more or that will be the last of the sandwich you taste.'

Fingle quickly swallowed, and spoke again.

'It's the cheese lust. It comes on those what 'ave taken the Jollop.'

'What do you mean?'

'A desire for cheese, a mad craving. The cheese lust!'

'Are you sure?'

'Yes. Old Snatcher has been working on it for years. He found some old book of cheese fables in his collection and started researching it. He found more and more stories about some plant that had wonderful effects on illnesses but cursed those that it cured with the cheese lust. So he got hold of some of this plant and set about his experiments. He was dosing up all kinds of animals with stuff and most of them went bonkers. But his favourite was the dogs. Once he dosed them up they made the best cheese hounds, but right vicious. We had to keep them muzzled. They would do anything for a whiff of cheese. Then a while ago he had a bit of a run in with you lot and he had to start out again. He had the bright idea that if could get everybody to take the stuff there would be so much demand for cheese that it would have to be decriminalized and he would get rich in the cheese trade again.'

'And the Spa was just a way to get people to take this evil substance?'

*'Once he dosed them up they made the best cheese hounds, but right vicious'*

'You got it right. Now give me the sandwich!'

'Just one last thing. Are we off to collect more of this plant he needs, then?'

'Yes, it only grows on one island on the whole planet.'

Willbury threw the sandwich on the floor in disgust. 'Let him have it.'

Fingle's guard released him, and the man fell upon the sandwich. In a trice it was gone.

'What shall we do with him now?'

'Lock him in the bilges.'

Fingle was taken off and those that remained stood in silence. Snatcher had again proved himself the most evil of men.

'I suggest we turn the ship about right away,' said Willbury. 'We cannot countenance delivering more of this evil substance to our fair country.'

'Hear! Hear!'

Then it struck Arthur. HIS GRANDFATHER HAD BEEN POISONED!

'Grandfather! What are we going to do? He's been poisoned! We have to cure him!'

'I'm not sure what we can do.' The realization of what they had just learnt was sinking in, and the group looked miserable.

'There may not be a cure,' Arthur muttered. 'Then what?'

'Ask Snatcher?' said Kipper who had joined them. 'We have got him in a bit of a corner.'

'I doubt he is going to help us with this. But we can try.'

'What else can we do?' said Willbury.

'I've a few ideas,' Bert added darkly.

They trooped up to the stern and used the stick to knock on the window of the cabin below. A very sleepy face looked out through the window.

'What is it?'

'We want to speak to Snatcher.'

'I'll go and get him.'

Snatcher appeared. 'What do you want now?'

Willbury looked down in contempt. 'We know what you have been up to with your Black Jollop.'

Snatcher looked startled. 'How? You been spying through walls?'

'Never you mind. We know everything. Your poisoning of the ill, the cheese lust, and how you intended to start up the cheese trade again.'

'Blooming Henry! You do know it all.' Then a dark look crossed his face. 'It was that Fingle. I'll have 'im.'

*'It was that Fingle. I'll have 'im.'*

 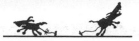 

'Never mind that. We need you to help us cure everybody.'

'You must be joking. Even if I end up back in prison, when I get out the demand for cheese will still be so high it will be easy to get it legalized again. That Jollop is permanent. That is the beauty of it. So many have taken the cure that using my cheese knowledge and contacts I will come the richest man in the land.'

Marjorie spoke. 'You are disgusting!'

Snatcher just laughed.

'And there is no cure for the cheese lust?'

'NO!' Snatcher scoffed.

All the windows of the captain's cabin were now open and filled with heads.

'You will never profit by this. I will make sure that you and that doctor of yours will never get out of prison.'

'Even if I have to live out my days in jail, just the thought of that cheesy desire will be enough to keep me going,' snapped Snatcher. 'It's a very sweet revenge for what Ratbridge has done to me.'

'You're mad!' said Willbury and Snatcher rolled his eyes.

Marjorie noticed that the doctor had been watching all that had been going on and seemed to be trying to catch her attention without being noticed by Snatcher.

When he saw that Marjorie had seen him he clearly mouthed 'I can help'. She turned and led the group away from the rail.

'I think the doctor wants to talk to us. He was signalling to me when Willbury was talking to Snatcher.'

'Wants to save his own skin.'

'Maybe, but why would he be signalling to me?' Marjorie wondered.

'Let's find out. Ask him.'

'Don't do that. If he's down there, and turns on Snatcher, Snatcher will do him in. No. We have to get him out somehow.'

'How do we do that?' asked Kipper.

'He's a doctor, isn't he. Tell Snatcher that someone is ill and needs a doctor,' suggested Arthur.

'Brilliant idea.'

They returned to the rail.

'We want a favour from you.'

'Do you really!' laughed Snatcher.

'Yes. We need a doctor. One of the crew has got a very large boil.'

'I am glad to hear it. Why should I help you lot?'

'I might go a little easier on you in court if you show some compassion,' answered Willbury.

Snatcher weighed up the situation. 'Very well. You are welcome to him. Fat lot of good it will do you. He is useless as a doctor. When I found him he was reduced to working as a receptionist at a vet's.'

The crew lowered a rope and hauled up the doctor. As soon as he was over the rail he spoke.

 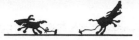

'There isn't a real boil, is there? I can't stand them. They make me go funny just looking at them.'

'No. No. Why were you trying to get my attention?'

The doctor looked round at Willbury. 'If I can help you will you drop charges against me?'

Willbury looked distrustful. 'It would have to be some very real help, and I still might not be able to promise you anything. But remember if you don't it could be life in clink!'

'Well, I think there might be a cure for the cheese lust.'

*'There isn't a real boil is there?'*

*'In my spare time I'd do hair-related experiments'*

Chapter 25

# The Doctor's Story

'I didn't start out with the intention of being a crook. My father was a doctor, as was his father before him, and my mother had her heart set on me being one as well. I started my medical training in Edinburgh and at first it went very well. Then I fell in with what I can only call "a bad set".

'I'd developed an interest in hair and everything about it. The chemical composition of different colours, the way it grew, how to make it grow, everything! I still find it fascinating. In my spare time I'd do hair-related experiments and slowly my experiments took over my life. I stopped attending lectures and seldom went out apart from to the barbers to collect sweepings. I became more and more obsessed with male early-onset baldness. I knew if I could

understand it I might be able to find a cure and that would make my name and fortune.

'In the early autumn of my third year I discovered certain chemical changes in the scalps and hair of those becoming rapidly bald and I knew I was on to something. But there was a problem. I needed hair samples and I needed them from the very men who least liked giving it up. Those going prematurely bald!

'In my desperation I turned to drink and one night in a bar I met two very unsavoury characters. I fell into conversation with them and told them about my work. Strangely they seemed very interested, and after a few more drinks said they might be able to help me with my studies. I asked how as they both had a very full head of hair and they told me it was better not to ask. Before I left I gave them my card and thought nothing more of it.

'Then a few days later there was a knock at my door. I was surprised, but as the rent wasn't due I answered it. Before me were the men I'd met in the bar.

'I wasn't sure why they had come to visit me, and not having had a drink they seemed even less appealing. I asked them what they wanted and they told me they had something for me.'

'What was it?' asked Arthur.

'Fresh hair from a balding man! They produced a small folded piece of newspaper and unwrapped it to reveal a pile of fine ginger hair. Now I've not mentioned this, but ginger hair is the highest in the chemicals I was seeking so my delight was intense and I offered to pay the men well. The men then said that the hair was a free sample, and more could be provided whenever I wanted. With that they left their cards and were gone.'

*'They produced a small folded piece of newspaper and unwrapped it to reveal a pile of fine ginger hair'*

Willbury had raised a hand. 'Sir, let me ask you their names?'

The doctor looked ashamed. 'Their names, sir, were Broadwood and Widger.'

'I thought they might be.'

Arthur was astonished that Willbury knew the names of the men and was about to ask how, but Willbury signalled to him to stay quiet and allow the doctor to continue his story.

'I was very thankful for this supply of new hair and it proved to be the best sample I had ever analysed. But soon it was gone in the flurry of experiments that it allowed. So I

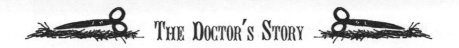

went to see Mr Broadwood. I found him at home in a small but luxurious house not too far from the centre of the city. When he saw me at the door he pulled me in quickly and then offered me tea.

'"I suppose you need more hair?" he asked.

'I admitted that this was indeed why I'd come and asked if he could supply me again. He replied that he could but this time there would be a cost. Fourteen groats was the sum. A huge amount in those days, but I had my allowance from my parents so I agreed.

'A few days later the hair arrived and again it was of beautiful quality. I worked for several days and again the hair was used up. So again I visited Broadwood.

'Over the next few weeks I spent more than two hundred groats, just on hair. But *what* hair! My experiments were starting to bear fruit and then . . . it happened.

'Needing more hair, I set off late one evening to collect another batch from Broadwood. As I left his house I can only have walked a few yards when I suddenly felt a hand on my collar.

'"I am arresting you under the 1738 Trading in Illegally Gathered Scalps and Toenail Act."

'Oh, the shame of it! I was being arrested by members of the Edinburgh hair robbery squad. Deep down I knew that the hair I had been using must have been collected illegally but I had swept those thoughts away with the wonder of my scientific experiments.

*'I was being arrested by members of the Edinburgh hair robbery squad'*

'So yes, you guessed correctly Mr Nibble. Broadwood and Widger, the infamous hair robbers, had been my suppliers. They would go out at night, find drunken balding men, offer them spiked drinks and then when the men passed out shave off their last remaining hair.

'They got twenty years and transportation, while my family got me a very good lawyer and I got off with a ten groat fine and barring from the medical profession. After the trial my family cut off my allowance and disowned me. So I moved south and hid myself in the "job" that Snatcher mentioned. A receptionist at a vet's practice. That is where he found me.'

'What on earth was Snatcher doing going to a vet's?' asked Arthur.

'He turned up and asked if we had any spare animals. Thinking he was after something as a pet, I told him that the animals we had were mostly ill or very old. To my surprise this seemed to be exactly what he wanted. Then I asked him what type of animal he wanted and he said everything we had. At the vet's we always like to give homes to animals if we can so I offered to find out what we had and told him I could run them round to him later.

'When I turned up with the animals, my interest was raised when I saw much of the same equipment I had been using in my own experiment. I asked him about his work and we talked for hours about complex organic molecules and such things. Around midnight I made to leave and he asked me if I wanted a job. With no hesitation I said yes and the next day I started to help him with his work.'

'What were you doing?' asked Marjorie.

'Each day plants in parcels from around the world would turn up and we would crush them up and analyse them. He told me he was trying to find a fabled plant whose extract could cure almost all ills but which also had some very interesting side effects.'

*'We would crush them up and analyse them'*

'Who sent the plants?'

'Snatcher placed adverts in botanical magazines right

across the world. Thousands of samples came in but most had no healing effect at all.'

'How did you know?'

'We tested them on animals, usually with no effect . . . or at least no positive effect. But one day a package arrived with the seeds of a tree from the rainforests of some Pacific island. They were not like any I'd seen before, and when tested we found they were rich in new chemical compounds. Snatcher made up some pills from the refined compounds and fed it to a tiny puppy. The puppy hadn't been well but very, very quickly—in fact within a number of minutes—it was bright and breezy as anything.

'Snatcher kept the puppy under a close watch and on the third day noticed the dog was sniffing the air at lunchtime. From the larder Snatcher took a covered dish and lifted the lid. The very moment he did the little dog attacked him savagely. But instead of Snatcher being cross he seemed very happy. I didn't discover what had been in that dish until later.

*'Instead of Snatcher being cross he seemed very happy'*

'So we'd discovered a fabled cure. He wrote to the plant collector who'd forwarded the parcel to us and soon a much larger package arrived. We set about refining its contents and making a syrup so we could control the dosages.

'I did ask him about the behaviour of the puppy and he told me not to worry. I know now that it was the side effects that he wanted to exploit.

'Then we started human trials. The results were remarkable. No illness seemed able to resist our Black Jollop. Our patients were people Snatcher found in the villages around Ratbridge. After a few days one or two of them came back and Snatcher would see them alone. After these consultations the patient left contented so I left it at that.'

'And how did you learn the truth about the side effects?'

'One morning when I was working alone and I found a book on the work bench in our laboratory. There was a marker in its pages. So I sat with a cup of tea and read. The volume was a book of fairytales and legends featuring cheese.

*'The volume was a book of fairytale and legends featuring cheese'*

'Amongst the stories I found one that told of a distant island where a giant cabbage grew. Under its shade lived a happy people who used the tree for medicine, but found that it also made them crazy for cheese.'

The doctor turned to Marjorie. 'The point is, in the story the people took another plant to save them from the madness. So there might be a cure.'

'But that is just a storybook.'

'Yes, but it is that very same legend that told of our original plant as well.'

'True. I think you might have something,' said Marjorie.

'And you knew of the terrible side effect and still went along with Snatcher's plan. That is truly appalling,' Willbury snapped angrily at the Doctor.

'Yes. I'm afraid so. I just couldn't face the idea of returning to the vet's, so I kept my mouth closed and went along with him. As part of his plan there was the spa and I was given centre stage. I just couldn't resist it.'

'You are a truly awful man. You went along with Snatcher and his scheme knowing that it might be causing people harm. Shocking! Didn't you swear the Hippocratic oath?' Willbury asked.

The doctor dropped his gaze to the floor, looking very ashamed.

Arthur had listened very hard and now wanted an answer to his own question. 'So you think that the plant in the story that cures the lust is real?'

'Yes I do. It all adds up.'

'In evolution there is quite often a symbiotic relationship between one organism that is poisonous and another that has learnt to live alongside it that produces an antidote or anti-venom,' added Marjorie.

'Well, if that is the case I guess we have to go to the island to see if we can find the cure.'

'No doubt about it.'

The doctor then looked a little worried. 'What do you want me to do?'

'I think you'd better join Fingle in the bilges. Snatcher is going to wonder why we are still heading towards the island and may guess you've told us something.'

As the doctor was taken off Arthur spoke to Marjorie. 'Do you think it's true?'

'Yes I do. Now all we have to do is find that island.'

*'Now all we have to do is find that island'*

NOCENS SENTENTIA PRO IGNARUS

1 GROAT

# THE ·Ratbridge·Gazette·

# Cheese Conservationists Bring In New Breeding Stock!

Members of the RWCA are bringing in new cheeses to help rebuild the local population. We applaud this move, but ask 'Will our cheeses be the same?'

'The cheeses we're importing are from South Wales and while paler and not so well scented, are close biological cousins of our local cheeses and should breed easily with them.'

*The sea became very rough*

## Chapter 26

# SOUTH TO THE HORN

Even running with full sail and the boiler steaming twenty-four hours a day, it took another week for the ship to reach Cape Horn. As the ship sailed south, it became colder, and colder, and the sea became very rough. Arthur had not really thought very much about how the ship might hold up to high winds and weather, but now he was amazed by how well she coped with the huge rolling seas. The crew were also showing what fine sailors they were under their captain Tom.

As the weather worsened it became increasingly difficult to work out their position. There was no sun for Marjorie to make a reading from, and but she knew they must be very close to the coast of Patagonia. She was constantly nervous and jumpy, as there was the danger that they could run aground at any time, and frustratingly little she could do to make sure they stayed safe.

Then came an albatross. The crew spotted her gliding just feet over the surface of the giant rollers. Soon she was flying alongside them, barely moving her vast wings as she did.

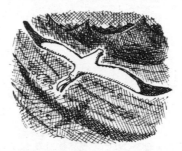

*Gliding just feet over the surface of the giant rollers*

'Bit windy, isn't it!' she called.

'Yes!' shouted Tom through cupped hands.

'We must be mad to be out in this!'

'Yes!' yelled Tom again.

'Where are you going?'

'To the Pacific—we hope. We haven't been able to get a good bearing because of the weather.'

'Yes, it's terrible. Always is around here.'

'And I thought the weather in England was bad,' muttered Kipper from under his sou'wester. The wind was so strong now that it felt as if it was blowing the rain right into his skin.

'Well, must love you and leave you!' called the albatross cheerily. With the tiniest movement of her wings, she wheeled

to the right and started to swoop out across the waves.

Marjorie looked up suddenly from the chart she was studying. 'Before you go!' she shouted after the disappearing bird.

For a moment it seemed as if Marjorie's call would be lost in the wind, but then the albatross glided back round towards them.

'Yes?'

'Are we going in the right direction?'

'No.'

'WHAT!'

'No, you want to go directly south for about fifty miles. Otherwise you'll bump into land.'

'OH!' shouted Marjorie, looking rather stunned. 'Thank you!'

'No problem. Have a nice day!' And with that the albatross was off over the waves and gone.

Tom turned the ship directly south guided by the compass on the bridge, and they sailed on until Marjorie thought it was safe to turn west.

*Tom turned the ship directly south*

A day later the weather finally cleared enough for Marjorie to take a reading and she announced they were indeed in the Pacific and it would be safe to head north-west towards their destination.

Arthur spent most of his time with Willbury below deck, as the rolling seas and strong winds had grown very tiring, but to everybody's surprise Fish was now spending every moment he could on deck. It didn't matter what the weather was like. Fish was always there. And when he was not by the wheel he was to be seen standing on the bow and leaning into the wind. He seemed to have fallen in love with the ocean. When Kipper had first noticed this he disappeared for a few hours and returned on deck with an oilskin box cover he'd made for Fish. This Fish now wore proudly as he took on the elements.

*He was to be seen standing on the bow and leaning into the wind*

Onwards they ran and the weather became better with each mile further north they travelled. Marjorie spent a lot of time looking at the maps as she was trying to make sure they wouldn't miss the small island. Then one evening she came to Tom as he stood by the wheel.

'I think that we'll be in sight of the island by tomorrow afternoon.'

'Good,' said Tom. 'Just in time too as we've almost run out of fuel. I've enjoyed being back at sea, but I shall be very happy to have my feet on solid earth again.'

'Have you thought what we're going to do with Snatcher and his mob when we get there?'

'Yes . . . they're a real problem. But it's not just them. What about the trotting badgers?'

'I know. Once we're in shallow waters within reach of the island, Snatcher and his mob will be able to escape out of the window. It might be better to get them somewhere we can keep them under guard,' suggested Marjorie.

'We could stick them under the forecastle where we store the sails!'

'That would work. There are no windows in the sail store,' agreed Marjorie.

Tom rubbed his head. 'There is still the problem of getting them out of their cabin and up here. The trotting badgers are blocking the stairs to the cabin.'

'We could haul them up in the net over the stern.'

'I think you have forgotten one thing. Snatcher's men still

have their weapons,' said Tom. 'And I doubt they'll agree to just giving them up and becoming our prisoners.'

Bert had been listening and suddenly perked up. 'Well, there may be a way round that.'

'What?' asked Kipper.

*'What?' asked Kipper*

'Remember that old saying about keeping your powder dry? Let's get out the hose and power up the bilge pump again.'

'You mean dampen their ardour!' giggled Marjorie.

'Not half,' chuckled Bert.

'I don't understand?' asked Tom.

'If we can get their gunpowder wet, their guns will be useless.'

'But they're down below and we're up here. How do we get their gunpowder wet?'

'Holes!'

'What do you mean?'

'Get Kipper and Arthur up here and have them sort out the pump and hose. I'll go and get me toolkit.'

By the time Bert returned to the bridge, Kipper and Arthur were dragging the end of the hose up from the deck. Bert opened his toolbox and took out a bit and brace.

'This should do the trick.' He started to drill holes through the planking of the bridge, down through the ceiling of the captain's cabin.

*He started to drill holes through the planking*

'We can block these holes up with corks and tar later.'

The wood of the deck was thick and very hard but after an hour there were about twenty holes spread over the deck.

'Start the pump!' shouted Bert as he pushed the hose into the first of the holes.

*'Start the pump!'*

Arthur heard cries from below as the water shot down into the cabin.

'Have to move it about a bit and surprise them. We need to get everything nice and wet down there,' said Bert as he jumped from hole to hole with the hose. After about ten minutes of screaming from below even Bert thought that it had probably worked.

'Turn off the pump. I think their ardour is sufficiently dampened.'

Marjorie took the long stick and knocked on the cabin window. A very wet and disgruntled Snatcher appeared.

'What was that for?'

'Thought you might need a wash,' laughed Bert.

Snatcher gave Bert a very nasty look but didn't say anything.

Now that Snatcher was suitably softened up Marjorie spoke. 'We are offering you the chance to co-operate with us.'

'And if we don't?'

'Would you like another wash?'

'NO! We'll co-operate.'

'OK. We'll haul you all up and put you somewhere safe away from the badgers. If you don't try anything we won't harm you.'

Bert and a lot of the larger crew members had armed themselves with old swords and clubs, and acted as guards as Snatcher and his men were lifted up over the stern and

escorted to the sail store. Once the prisoners were inside the door was bolted and locked.

As night fell the sky cleared and a warm westerly breeze came up.

'We are all set for the island,' said Marjorie as she finished taking a reading from the Southern Cross.

*Escorted to the sail store*

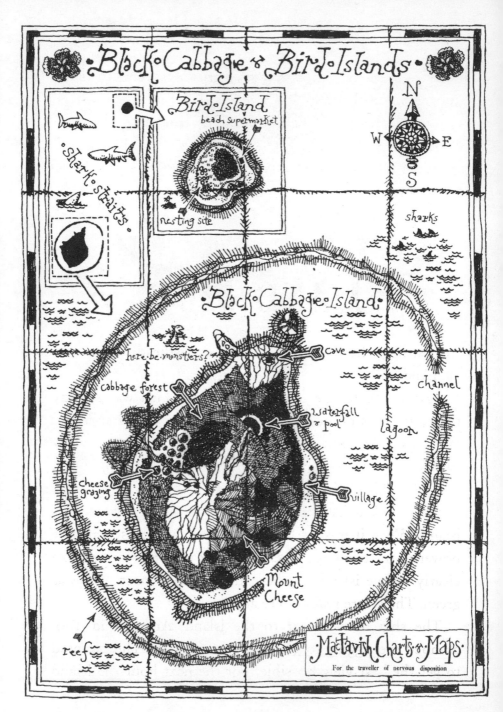

*Arthur followed Fish's gaze and saw a tiny speck*

## Chapter 27

# LAND HO!

At first light there was a cry from the masthead.

'Land ho!'

Arthur ran to the forecastle to look. Fish was already there, and was pointing into the distance. Arthur followed Fish's gaze. Straining to see, he could just make out a tiny speck, but it was too far away to see what it was. Kipper arrived to join them carrying a large telescope.

They took it in turns to have a look at the approaching island. When it was Arthur's turn he was surprised at how powerful the telescope was. The speck was transformed to a clearly visible island and he could see that most of it was green. They were really there at last!

The ship drew closer to the island. Arthur and Tom climbed the rigging to get to the crow's nest. They wanted to get the best view possible. For the next hour the island grew bigger. As they got closer Arthur could see waves rising and breaking some distance from the island.

'Why are the waves breaking before they reach the island?'

'Quite often there is a ring of coral that runs around islands. It's called a reef and the waves break when they hit it,' said Tom.

'Well, how do we get to the island then?'

'If the sea bed is uneven there can be a break in the reef. We'll have to look out for one, as there may only be one place we can get through.'

Arthur scanned the breaking waves and saw that there was indeed a place where the waves didn't seem to be breaking. He pointed it out to Tom.

'There!'

'Very good, Arthur.' Tom called down to the deck. 'There is a break in the reef.'

*'There is a break in the reef.'*

'What direction?' called back Kipper, who was now on the wheel.

'Ten degrees to starboard.'

Kipper changed course and made for the passage.

Then Arthur spotted two of the crew on the forecastle, each dropping weights on ropes on either side of the bow.

'What are they doing?'

'Checking the depth of the water,' said Tom. 'We don't know these waters and could run aground. The ropes have knots in them six feet apart. Six feet is called a fathom, and they call out the number of fathoms when the weight hits the sea bed.'

He watched the sailors checking how much line they were paying out each time they dropped the weights, then calling back to Kipper.

Kipper continued steering the ship towards the break and instructed the crew to lower some of the sails.

At about a hundred yards from the break Kipper ordered the rest of the sails to be dropped. The ship slowed and slid smoothly through the gap in the reef. From Arthur's position up in the crow's nest he could see the reef under the water, stretching out in a ring parallel to the beach. Inside the reef the waters became very calm and the ship moved almost silently towards the shore.

Arthur looked towards the island. A thick green canopy started after a wide sandy beach. Arthur gazed into the jungle. Somewhere in there was the plant they needed! Arthur felt a bubble of excitement start up inside him. At last it seemed that they would really be able to find the antidote and cure everyone who had been poisoned by the Black Jollop—including Grandfather!

As the ship drew closer into land, more and more of the crew gathered on the deck below them.

'I think we had better get down there too,' said Tom. 'We don't want to be last in.'

'Last in?'

'Yes, as soon as the anchor is dropped, anybody who hasn't got a job to do has to jump in the sea. It's a bit of a tradition.'

The ship had slowed almost to a stop a few hundred yards from the beach when Kipper called for the anchor to be dropped. As the anchor found a hold on the seabed the ship slowly swung its bow into the wind and came to rest. Then there was a cry.

'Last one in is a mouldy old goat!'

Arthur and Tom were still some way up the rigging when the cry went out, and they stopped for a moment to watch as bodies flung themselves over the side.

'I think we'd better jump from here if we're not to be last in,' said Tom.

He then took a leap and shouted 'Geronimo!' as he plummeted into the bright blue water. Arthur was not so sure. He kept climbing down, trying to pluck up the courage to jump.

'Come on, Arthur!' shouted Tom. 'There's hardly anyone left to jump!'

Screwing up his courage, Arthur leapt and, following Tom's lead, shouted 'Geronimo'. He hit the water and was surprised at how warm it was. As he surfaced he saw the faces of friends all around him.

Then somebody shouted. 'Kipper is an old goat!'

Everybody in the water turned to look. Kipper had appeared in a strange orange and blue knitted bathing suit and was about to jump from the side of the ship.

'Always last.' It was Tom, who was a few feet from Arthur in the water.

Kipper jumped and there was another cheer. Then Arthur noticed Fish standing on the handrail at the side of the ship. He couldn't believe his eyes. The boxtroll jumped!

For a second the boxtroll disappeared below the water but then bobbed straight to the surface.

'I can't believe it!'

Tom spoke. 'Thought that would surprise you. Kipper filled all the spare space inside his box with corks. Now he will float like one.'

Arthur laughed and swam over to Fish. He had never seen Fish look so happy. The boxtroll was now paddling around gurgling and wailing with joy, and even splashed at Arthur as he came close.

'You've changed!'

Fish nodded and splashed some more.

'Very good Fish. You really are living up to your name,' Willbury called from the rail of the ship.

*He had never seen Fish look so happy*

'Come on in and join us,' Arthur called back.

'No, no, no. I shall leave it to you young ones to enjoy the waters. I had a good wash this morning.'

'When do we go ashore?' Arthur asked Tom.

'I think we'll leave it until tomorrow. It mightn't be wise to go into the jungle just as it gets dark.'

As the sun went down the crew set fishing lines off the sides of the ship and soon had enough for supper. The boiler still had enough heat in it to cook the fish and in a few minutes everybody was tucking in. The crew even passed some through the bars to Snatcher and his mob.

*The boiler still had enough heat in it to cook the fish*

Arthur sat with Willbury and Fish as they tucked in.

'Be interesting to see what happens tomorrow.'

'Yes, Arthur. I hope we do find the plants we are looking for. There is a chance we won't. God alone knows what's on that island.'

This they were to discover first thing the following morning. The night had been very dark but as the sun broke over the horizon it silhouetted the shape of a huge lizard walking towards the ship.

On deck Kipper and Bert saw it at the same time and let out a huge scream.

'WHAT IS IT?'

The monster moved closer.

*'WHAT IS IT?'*

NOCENS SENTENTIA PRO IGNARUS

1 GROAT

# THE ·Ratbridge·Gazette·

# Welsh Cheeses Eaten!

This morning tearful members of the RWCA reported that all imported Welsh cheeses seem to have been eaten.

'It seems they were easy prey. Even though they have not fared so well in recent times our local cheeses have a certain cunning and speed. The Welsh cheeses were pale and rather weak so were very vulnerable. When our newly appointed cheese warden went out to inspect them this morning there were none left.'

When asked what was to be the next move to save our cheeses, the RWCA spokesman shrugged his shoulders and muttered that they might have to consider stronger foreign cheeses.

This paper says, 'DO WE WANT FOREIGN CHEESE?'

*'You've got to get out!'*

## Chapter 28

# MONSTER!

The monster was huge . . . and coming straight towards them. Everyone started panicking.

'What are we going to do?'

'I . . . I don't know. That thing is coming straight at us and it doesn't look friendly.'

'Load up the cannon?'

'It would be like firing a peashooter at an elephant!'

'How about every man for himself! Swim for the shore!'

'Is swimming for the shore a good idea?' asked Marjorie. 'That monster has come from the island, after all—who knows what else might be lurking on there?'

Tom looked thoughtful. 'You are right . . . but I don't think we have any choice! If we stay on the ship we are just sitting ducks. I'm going to give the order to make for the island.'

'What about Snatcher and his men?' pointed out Arthur.

'They're locked in the sail store.'

Everyone looked at the door. There was no time to think.

'I think we had better let them out? If not . . . '

'Are you sure you don't just want to leave them to their fate?' Bert asked.

'No. We can't be that heartless. Let them out.'

Reluctantly Bert unlocked the door.

'You've got to get out!'

'Why?'

'There's a monster about to attack us. If you want to save yourselves swim for the shore.'

It took a few moments for the news to sink in and then Snatcher spoke again.

'I don't believe you.'

'All of you! Come out here and have a look.'

They did as they were told and looked towards where the crew were staring.

'Blooming Henry! Swim for your lives!'

A stream of Snatcher's men followed him over the side and started to make for the beach.

'OK! Abandon ship!' ordered Tom. 'And Kipper, you'd better go and let Fingle and the doctor free.'

Kipper rushed below deck, returned with the bilge residents, and with rather too much enthusiasm 'helped' them over the side.

Arthur felt a hand on his shoulder.

'I can't swim.' It was Willbury.

Arthur looked about the deck for something that would float and spotted the apple barrel.

'Kipper, Marjorie! Give me a hand.'

They managed to roll the barrel across the deck and lower it over the side so it floated mouth up in the water. Then they helped Willbury climb down and into the barrel.

'We'll be able to push him along with us.'

'OK,' shouted Kipper, and joined Arthur and the others as they jumped into the sea.

'Push!'

Arthur looked towards the monster. It was only about 200 yards from the ship and closing fast. The barrel was moving very slowly.

'Push harder!' he cried.

*'Push harder!'*

'Thank you for saving me,' came a weak voice from inside the barrel.

No one was left on the ship apart from the trotting badgers, but the sea was filled with very energetic swimmers. Between strokes everybody was keeping an eye on the lumbering monster.

It reached the ship and stopped. Its enormous eyes scanned the decks. Then it slowly looked to left and right in the sea.

'It's seen us!'

Arthur watched as the enormous head turned towards them. It opened its huge wide mouth and revealed tombstone-sized teeth.

Screaming mixed with the sound of the waves.

*It opened its huge wide mouth and revealed tombstone-sized teeth.*

*Inside the brain of the monster there was confusion*

## Chapter 29

# MONSTROUS THOUGHTS

Inside the brain of the monster there was confusion.

'What are we going to do now?'

'Tell the neck to turn from side to side, and have the eyes look about and report back.'

'They have all jumped in the sea and are swimming for the beach,' came the message from the eyes.

'I think we've really scared them.'

'We'll have to pick them up out of the water. Open up the mouth and bend over a little bit.'

The escaping swimmers were within easy reach of a quick snap and were starting to panic.

There was a certain amount of worry inside the monster's head as well.

'If we don't start grabbing them out of the water we are going to lose some of them. Bend over more!'

'OK, jaws, when you are in position start swallowing, and try not to take in too much water.'

Arthur watched in horror as the monster struck. Its mouth lowered over three trailing swimmers and closed.

'Push Willbury faster or it will get us!'

The monster tipped its head back and swallowed. Then leant forward again for another mouthful.

*The monster tipped its head back and swallowed*

In the stomach the first of the screaming swimmers arrived.

'Aaaaaargh!'

Then they hit the stomach floor.

Boing! Boing! Boing!

'Uh?'

'What's going on?'

'I can't see anything.'

'Are we dead?'

'No. I don't think so. In fact I feel all right apart from being eaten by a monster.'

'Me too. Did you bounce?'

'Yes.'

'Me too.'

'What happens now?'

'I don't think it's so good. We get digested. Something like that. I should've listened more at school.'

*'I should've listened more at school'*

Then they covered their heads as they heard more screaming from above and a few moments later they were joined by the next mouthful.

Arthur could not bear to look back. They could hear the monster behind them and this gave the spur to swim as hard as they could. Slowly the screaming behind them grew less as more and more swimmers were swallowed, until Arthur guessed they were the last.

'Faster! We're almost at the beach.'

'Whatever happens, I just want you to know you've all been good friends to me,' Kipper spluttered.

A shadow fell over them and Arthur felt something lifting them from the water.

'GOODBYE, ARTHUR!' shouted Willbury, just before the monster's jaws closed around them all.

*'GOODBYE, ARTHUR!'*

1 GROAT

# THE ·Ratbridge·Gazette·

# BANGED TO RIGHTS

In a raid on the Ratbridge Women's Guild this afternoon twenty-seven women were arrested. Cheese hounds led the police to a church hall where the women were found in possession of shards of cheese. None of the 'Cheesy Crimesses' denied it, instead claiming not to have been able to control themselves. Do we believe this? NO! Send them down!

*'Whoever has got his knee in my ear, will you kindly shift it!'*

## Chapter 30

# GUTTED!

'Well done, jaws. I think we've got the lot of them.'

'Back to the beach?'

'I think we better had. Our stomach is so full I think we might not be able to eat for a week.'

There was some laughing inside the head and the creature made for the beach.


'Whoever has got his knee in my ear, will you kindly shift it!' demanded Kipper.

'And whoever's sitting on my head will you please shift your butt!' This time Arthur recognized Snatcher's voice from immediately below him.

'Sorry.' Arthur moved himself to cause less moaning. Then the stomach start to shake and quiver.

'We're moving!'

The creature walked slowly across the lagoon and up the beach.

A message went out from the eyes. 'OK. We are on dry land!'

On receiving this information a command went out from the head to the legs to stop.

The feet of the monster settled in the sand and the creature came to rest.

Inside the stomach the monster's breakfast fell silent. Arthur's face was pressed against a warm rubbery wall. He heard something through it. At first he wasn't sure what it was, but slowly he realized it was muffled talking.

The wall moved just above his head, pushing against him, and then a hole appeared. Daylight rushed in and a split zipped down past him.

Arthur found himself falling along with the rest of the stomach's contents on to the beach. It took a few moments before his eyes became used to the sunlight, then he heard something he didn't quite believe.

'Sorry about that. We didn't mean to scare you. But once we had, the quickest way to stop anybody drowning was to eat you.'

Surrounding them were about a hundred rather large and very apologetic looking people. They all had soft brown skin, and wore brightly coloured wraps of cloth.

A big woman walked forward towards the pile of bodies.

*Arthur found himself falling, along with the rest the stomach's contents, on to the beach*

'We're very sorry, but we usually spot any ships before they arrive and can scare them away.'

Arthur looked from the woman to the monster behind them. He wasn't quite sure what to expect but it didn't look so scary now. In fact it didn't look scary at all. More like a lot of scaffolding wrapped in old dirty sheets.

'It's not real!' Arthur exclaimed.

'That's right.'

'Did you make it?'

The large woman smiled. 'Yes . . . well I say yes, our people made it a couple of hundred years ago when the ships started to arrive and cause trouble. We just keep it going to stop outsiders bothering us. Worked pretty well up until now.'

'You're speaking English!' exclaimed Marjorie.

This had not struck Arthur until this point, but now it did seem odd.

'Yes. Let me explain, but first I would like to formally introduce myself and welcome you to our island. I'm Queen Florence but you can all call me Flo.'

She bowed and the contents of the monster's stomach struggled to their feet to return the greeting.

Then the queen went on. 'We hoped you might be English as we find the language so poetic. We learnt it from a sailor who got washed up here. Quite often when we have a day off we will practise it.'

'You seem to speak excellent English, ma'am,' said Willbury.

'Thank you. I try to learn as many languages as I can. It really helps to understand the cultures. What languages do you speak?'

There was an embarrassed silence from the English speakers in front of her.

'Oh well. You should try it. Our own language is very beautiful for doing maths and sciences but doesn't have so many fancy words for art and romance. Now I have a question. Why have you come here?'

There was a silence while the shipmates looked at each other rather awkwardly.

'Thank you for your welcome.' Willbury took the lead, as no one else seemed to want to. 'It's a long story but it can be put down to some of us wanting to cure some people, while others here want to poison them.'

'And which of you are which?'

The crew separated themselves from Snatcher and his mob, leaving the doctor and Fingle standing between them. Then, seeing the look on Snatcher's face, both Fingle and the doctor moved to join the crew.

Willbury pointed at Snatcher's group. 'These characters have poisoned some of our townsfolk with a potion that drives them crazy with a desire for cheese. We believe they got the ingredient from a plant from this island and that in order to cure our people we need to get another plant that grows here.'

Queen Flo looked very concerned. 'I think I know what you're talking about. The Black Cabbage Tree and the Un-cabbage Flower. But how did this happen? I didn't know anybody had taken any Cabbage Tree seeds away.'

A man standing next to the queen broke in. 'I bet it's Guillemot, and the mob from Shopping Island. You just can't trust them.'

*Guillemot*

There was much nodding of heads and muttering from the islanders.

'Who're they?' asked Willbury.

The man standing by the queen's side spoke again. 'There is an island five miles north of here where a people very unlike us live. It's very strange but they live to shop. We try not to have much to do with them but on occasion they do turn up. They're a right bunch!'

'Yes,' added the queen. 'On this island things are pretty perfect. We've everything we need to live on, and plenty of spare time to play and think. On their island they have everything they need too, but spend most of their time trying to outdo each other, by selling or shopping. It's very sad.'

'And this man Guillemot?'

'Guillemot is a trader. He turned up on their island and fitted right in. Ships visit their island occasionally and he organizes trading between the islanders and the ships.'

'And the ships never visit here because of your monster?'

'That's right.'

'Does your monster keep the islander  from the other island away as well?

'Not really. They knew about us building the monster and don't say anything because I think it suits them that people visit them instead of us.'

'And you've met this Guillemot?'

'Yes. He's been over here a few times trying to get us to

trade with him but we're not interested. Last time he was over he came when some others needed our medicine and he charged them for a ride in his boat. So Guillemot probably knows about our seeds. I'm guessing he must have stolen some, and is in part responsible for your Cabbage Tree poisoning.'

Willbury looked at Snatcher, who was looking very ill at ease. 'Is that so?'

*Willbury looked at Snatcher, who was looking very ill at ease*

Snatcher smirked.

'I'll take that as a yes then.' Willbury looked back at the Queen. 'Do you think you can help us?'

'Certainly! If your people have been poisoned by our Black Cabbage Tree, it is down to us to help put things right. It may take a few nights to collect the Un-Cabbage Flowers but then you will be able to cure the mania.'

'Thank you,' said Arthur. 'My grandfather is going to need some.'

'You mean to say that they've been poisoning old people?' Queen Flo was outraged and stared at Snatcher in disbelief. The crowd around her started to look very angry.

'Yes he has. He got everybody he could to take his poison, and he wanted to come here to get more seeds so he could poison more,' said Arthur.

'And how many people in total has he poisoned?'

'It must be at least several hundred.'

'Shocking! We'll start collecting this tonight. The only time you can pick the Un-Cabbage Flowers is at night after the cabbage rain.'

Arthur and his friends looked very puzzled.

'Every evening there is a rain that falls in the forest and this washes the poison down from the Black Cabbage Trees. When this happens the Un-Cabbage Flowers start to produce the antidote and by morning the forest is safe again. If you need to make medicine to cure illnesses you need to collect Black Cabbage Tree seeds by day and then very carefully collect the Un-Cabbage Flowers by night. As we only need the Un-Cabbage Flowers we'll have to work at night. Now tell me about this horrid man,' she said, and pointed to Snatcher.

Between Arthur and the others they told the story. As soon as they had heard what had happened, the islanders offered to keep Snatcher and his men in a cave nearby.

'It's safe and they won't be able to get out. We used to use it to keep anybody who had the cheese mania before we discovered how to cure them with the Un-Cabbage Flowers.'

'So some of your people got poisoned?' asked Arthur.

'Yes. Occasionally somebody would get caught in the rain and end up having to be locked away.

'It was very sad. The cheeses who live in the forest here have no natural predators and are the only creatures not affected by the cabbage rain, but once a few people got the mania they were almost wiped out.'

*The cheeses who live in the forest*

If someone had been very carefully watching Snatcher at that moment, they would've seen him lick his lips and mutter to himself.

Willbury spoke. 'It would be a real blessing if you could help us. There are a few other things we need like food, fuel and fresh water, for the journey home.'

'No problem. And you're welcome to stay on the island while we get everything you need.'

'That's very kind of you.'

'Do you need to get anything from your boat?'

'Well we need to bring our water barrels ashore to fill . . . '

'Would you like to use our fishing boats, or you could use our monster?'

Willbury looked slightly panicked and spoke hurriedly. 'I think the fishing boats, if we may.'

Arthur was very disappointed by this. The chance to ride in the monster seemed very appealing.

'Boats it is then. If some of you would like to get on with that, our children can help the other members of your crew find water and food.'

The island children all nodded.

'And,' added the queen, 'would you all like to feast with us tonight before we collect Un-Cabbage Flowers?' Then she added, 'Apart from the poisoners, that is.'

Tom shot a triumphant look at Snatcher and stepped forward to speak. 'I think I can say on behalf of the non-poisoners that we would like to accept your offer of a feast.'

Everybody apart from Snatcher and his mob cheered.

'So shall we say a feast at about ten and afterward we shall start collecting Un-Cabbage Flowers?'

'YES!' came the cry.

The meeting broke up. Bert and some of the islanders set off to the cave with Snatcher and company, Kipper took a boat back to the ship with some fishermen to collect water barrels, Arthur and the other crew went off to collect food and wood with the children. The other islanders set about preparing for the feast.

Fish kept close to Arthur as they wandered into the trees. He kept looking up worriedly.

*Fish kept close to Arthur*

'You don't need to worry,' said a small girl. 'The Black Cabbage Trees don't start until much higher up the hill and it never rains until exactly ten o'clock. Down here are just bread fruit, bananas, coconuts and yams.'

This made Fish feel much happier. He didn't like the idea of cabbage rain one bit.

Over the next few hours a huge pile of food built up on the sands and Kipper returned in a fishing boat towing the empty water barrels behind it. The bigger pirates then took the barrels to a nearby waterfall that the children showed them and filled them up, before rolling them back to the beach.

*Rolling the barrels back to the beach*

When the queen saw how fast everything was being done she told them not to rush too much as it would take at least three days to collect the flowers they needed.

'This is an island. And you have to learn to move at our speed!' she joked.

This seemed very agreeable to everyone, and they decided they'd done enough and had a long swim in the waterfall pool. Fish was the first to dive in, followed by Arthur. As they swam under the base of the waterfall Fish was as happy as Arthur had ever seen him.

*A long swim in the waterfall pool*

NOGENS SENTENTIA PRO IGNARUS

1 GROAT

# THE ·Ratbridge·Gazette·

## Mass Arrests As Net Closes on 'Cheesy Crims'

Ratbridge gaol is now overflowing with 'Cheesy Crims' after a police operation last night. Retained cheese-hounds led police to over a hundred addresses and at most of these, traces of cheese were found. In total over 200 'Cheesy Crims' were apprehended.

Police stated that there could only be a few of the mob at large, and it is only a matter of days before cheese would be safe again.

Conditions inside the gaol are said to be terrible. This paper says 'SERVES THEM RIGHT'!

*'Get yer vests off and start unravelling them'*

## Chapter 31

# IN A HOLE

Snatcher seemed in a surprisingly good mood for a trapped man. Although the cave had not been used for many years, a certain number of 'things' had fallen into it and were piled up on the floor. He waited until the voices above had died away and then spoke.

'Things ain't going to end this way. I've got a plan. Gristle, collect up all these bones and bits of old stick. We are going to make a ladder.'

'How's we going to stick them together?'

Snatcher looked at his men. 'Get yer vests off and start unravelling them.'

Ratbridge had always been home to the string vest, and this garment was to be their saviour. But it was not without a cost—for what Snatcher hadn't quite banked on was the smell. Even the dowsing and swim in the sea hadn't done much to ease the personal odour of his mob.

But there was no way round it so, pinching his nose, Snatcher oversaw the construction of the ladder. The stench was almost overpowering, and by the time the ladder was ready he had nearly passed out.

'Right. Put it up against the wall.'

The ladder was six feet short of the surface.

'I think we need to build it up a bit,' suggested Gristle.

'I guess we do. Gristle and the rest of you louts, lie down!'

They lay down in a heap, and Snatcher repositioned the ladder. On top of the heap.

'Very good, lads. Keep still while I climb up.'

The sounds of pain echoed around the cave as Snatcher clambered up the heap and started up the ladder. Soon he reached the surface and looked back.

'Gristle, you next. And bring any spare string.'

Gristle pulled himself out from the pile and did as he was told. Then one by one, the person at the top of the pile lifted the ladder off themselves, and placed it back on the pile so they could then climb up. The pile grew shorter and shorter, and the ladder sunk lower and lower. The last few took some hoisting with string to get them up to the top.

'I think I'm broken,' Gristle moaned.

'Which bit of you?'

'All of me.'

'Shut up and follow me,' snapped Snatcher. 'With luck we're going to take a monster for a walk.'

'What do you mean?'

'We're going to visit my old trading partner Guillemot, and we are going to use that monster to get there.'

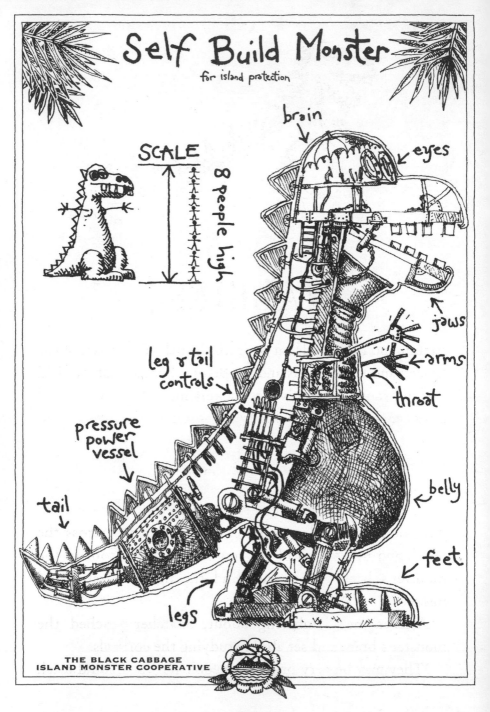

# Self Build Monster

for island protection

brain

eyes

SCALE

8 people high

jaws

arms

leg & tail controls

throat

pressure power vessel

belly

tail

feet

legs

THE BLACK CABBAGE
ISLAND MONSTER COOPERATIVE

*Shadowy figures rushed across the beach and up the tail of the monster*

## Chapter 32

# 'WALKIES!'

Arthur and his friends sat beneath the palms as guests of the Queen and the other islanders. Before them a feast was laid out and soon everybody was tucking into stone-pit-cooked pork, coconut milk cocktails and some of the finest food that Arthur had ever tasted. Everyone felt happy and optimistic—it looked as if their mission would soon be accomplished.

So engrossed were the party in their feast that they did not notice the shadowy figures rushing quietly across the beach and up the tail of the monster. A small door in the monster's back was opened and the figures disappeared inside.

After some clambering about, Snatcher reached the monster's brain and set about studying the controls.

'They may be very primitive people but they could teach

us a thing or two. Gristle, them's the levers what make the legs work. Start walkin'!'

Gristle did as he was told, there was some clunking, and the giant figure of the monster moved to the water's edge and started to paddle out to sea. Soon it had passed out of the lagoon and was waist-deep in seawater.

*Waist-deep in seawater*

'Master, some of 'em down below is getting very wet. Any chance we could get a bit shallower?'

'Tell 'em to hold their breath and remember the mutiny laws. I wouldn't want to have to chuck anybody out in these shark-infested waters.'

There were no more complaints.


Kipper had finished his third plate of ribs and sweet potato and Arthur had eaten at least two pineapples when Queen Flo arose to speak.

'We are going into the Cabbage Forest tonight not long after the rains. This we don't normally do, but we've a lot of flowers to collect. I'll issue you all with umbrellas to keep off any drips. Be careful! The ground will be wet and if you lick your toes it would be very dangerous. We'll go for a paddle in the sea afterwards to be on the safe side. Now please follow me.'

She led them to a hut stacked full of homemade umbrellas and everybody took one. They all formed a line with the Queen at its head and they set off into the darkness of the forest. Arthur could only just see Kipper in front of him in the gloom and he almost fell over a number of times as the ground was uneven and roots crossed the path. After a few minutes the Queen called out and the line stopped.

'It's about to start. Put up your umbrellas please.'

As they put them up Arthur asked, 'What is about to start?'

*The heavens opened*

But before anybody could answer him the heavens opened and the heaviest rain Arthur had ever encountered started. The noise was deafening and when the rain hit the ground it bounced almost to waist height.

Then as suddenly as it started . . . it stopped.

The air now felt very damp and warm, and there was a smell of vegetables.

'Does it do this every night?' Arthur asked.

'As regularly as the sun rises.'

'So is it safe now to start collecting the flowers?'

'NO! We have to wait until most of the dripping stops and even then there is a chance one of us could be poisoned. A single drip reaching your mouth would be enough . . . '

Arthur and his friends closed their mouths very tightly and made sure they were right under their umbrellas. The Queen saw their unease and smiled.

'It's safe where we're standing, but once I take you past the next stream the Black Cabbage trees start and you have to be very, very careful. Keep your umbrellas up and look for the purple flowers beneath the trees. If you find some, only pick one flower from each clump. That way they'll have a chance to grow back again.'

'How'll we see them in this dark?'

'You will, don't worry. Follow me!'

She led the nervous line over a stream towards the deadly dripping trees.

Arthur felt an umbrella bang into his from behind. It was Fish. The boxtroll was looking nervous, and obviously trying to stay as close as possible to Arthur.

Arthur considered reassuring his friend but instead decided to keep his mouth tight shut as every few seconds a light patter sounded as a drip landed on his umbrella.

Then something miraculous happened. Spots of pale purple light started to glow under the trees.

'Is that the flowers glowing?' Marjorie asked from between pursed lips.

'Yes. Beautiful, isn't it. They glow as they produce the antidote,' the Queen replied.

*'They glow as they produce the antidote'*

No one talked as they moved through the forest collecting the flowers. Arthur did get very scared when a breeze hit the trees above and a shower of drips rained down on his umbrella, but he managed to avoid any splashes.

Queen Flo collected the gathered flowers from everyone and when she thought they had enough led them quietly out of the forest and back to the beach for a paddle.

When their feet were washed of any poison, they walked up the beach and turned in for the night. New hammocks had been slung between the palm trees for the crew and it was a beautiful place to sleep.

'If things were different,' Arthur said to Willbury, 'it would the most perfect night in the whole world.'

Willbury agreed. 'It's not something I shall ever forget. Imagine *us* sleeping on a tropical island beach under the stars.'

The gentle breeze from the sea rustled the palm leaves above them, and the breaking of the waves lulled them slowly to sleep. It was glorious, and still no one noticed that the monster was gone.

NOCENS · SENTENTIA · PRO · IGNARUS

1 GROAT

# ·Ratbridge·Gazette·

## Trap Snaps on 'Cheesy Crims'!

Last night in a sting operation the police captured all but the very last of the 'Cheesy Crims'. Under the guidance of the RWCA a trap was baited with a humanely tethered cheese to capture the last of the miscreants that have been terrorizing our local cheeses. At around 9.15 p.m. a small mob headed towards the marshes in search of their poor victims, but were surprised when they fell into a covered pit. The police then tried to arrest the mob. In the melee one particularly evil 'Cheesy Crim' managed to escape.

'We chased him into the woods but he disappeared down a Trotting Badger hole, and escaped. We would have followed him, but it was felt that there was too great a risk of badger attack, so orders were given to hold back.

'We did however get a good look at him and have published a description.'

The man is described as sprightly, about 70 years old, some 5' 7" tall, with a thick beard, and wearing a tartan dressing gown with a woolly hat.

Here at the Gazette we are offering a reward of 2000 groats for the capture of this last blaggard.

*Guillemot's twenty-four hour beach supermarket*

## Chapter 33

# THE SUPERMARKET

Guillemot closed and locked the doors of the twenty-four hour beach supermarket at seven p.m. He'd had enough. It had been a hard day at the till and even with the mirrors placed around the store and a sharp eye, Guillemot had lost at least three shopping baskets, two boxes of postcards, and various other small items. This was not how he had thought his life on a south-sea paradise was going to be.

After a quick meal made up of the latest date-expired food items he climbed the steps to the roof. Here he would sit, watch the sun go down, and use the last of the light to prepare his catapult for anybody who tried to break in.

Once the sun set he relied on burglar-alarms and traps to dissuade the intruders. These worked so well that he'd not lost any stock for three nights.

Guillemot poured himself a large coconut cocktail and

sat back to wait for the first of the burglars. As he sipped he daydreamed of getting away from this miserable island, perhaps retiring to a little country cottage in England and never having to deal with shoplifters again. Then his attention turned to how the attack would come tonight.

'They're so unimaginative. I wish they would come up with something original.'

A bush moved slowly across the sands towards the supermarket.

'Not again!' he muttered as he took a coconut from a large pile by his sun-lounger and fired it at the bush. There was a scream and the bush ran away cursing.

*The bush ran away cursing*

'And I hope your nest is struck by lightning!' he called back.

He took another sip and sat back to wait for the next attempt. After his alarm had gone off three times, and he had emptied the trap pits twice he managed to get an hour's sleep.

Then something woke him. He felt uneasy, but was not

sure why as the alarms were silent and there were no signs of bushes.

He looked over the edge of his stockade. No one was trying to tunnel in, and the traps were empty.

'Something's up. I just know it.'

After wandering around the store he climbed back on the roof and sat down again. Then he saw it. Coming towards the island was the monster the cabbage islanders used to scare off outsiders.

'I wonder what they want?' Then he smiled. 'Maybe they want to buy something!' He put down his catapult and decided to go down to meet his possible customers.

The monster was on the beach and had come to a stop by the time Guillemot reached it. He was now rubbing his hands at the thought of making some money.

The small door opened and started to disgorge some highly disreputable-looking characters. Most of them were soaked through and gasping for breath—clearly they had spent impressive amounts of time under water while moving the monster through the sea. The largest and most ferocious-looking of them, a large man with an eye patch, had no such difficulties—he was not at all out of breath and was completely bone dry—obviously, Guillemot thought, he must have stayed well out of trouble in the head of the monster.

As the men gathered themselves and began to recover from their underwater ordeal, Guillemot stared. They weren't islanders! In fact they looked English. Yes, he was sure of it. The pale skin, the miserable look, the dirty ill-fitting clothes. Yes! They must be his countrymen.

He rushed forward.

'Excuse me. Are you English?'

The large man with the eye patch looked him up and down. 'Yes. And are you Guillemot of Guillemot's Fairtrade botanicals and knick-knacks?'

*'Are you Guillemot of Guillemot's Fairtrade botanicals and knick-knacks?'*

The islanders must have told these men of another of their countrymen. 'Yes, sir. And who am I addressing?'

'One of your customers. Archibald Snatcher esquire.'

Guillemot was shocked and not sure quite what to do. It crossed his mind that Archibald Snatcher esquire had come to complain—but he had sent him his order of Black Cabbage Seeds and the seeds really did what he said in his advertisements. He decided that it was best just to play along for the moment.

*'At your service.'*

'At your service,' said Guillemot, giving a bow. 'Your order? It did arrive safely?'

'Oh, yes.'

'And you were happy with it?'

'Very much so. We'd like some more, a lot more. So we thought we'd come in person. Deal direct if you get my meaning. But we have a few problems. I don't think the producers are going to co-operate with supplying our requirements. That is why we're here. We thought you might be able to help us.'

Snatcher gave Guillemot a wink with his good eye. 'I think we might need a bit of extra manpower to get things done.'

Guillemot was starting to get the picture. 'Did you "borrow" the monster?'

'Yes.'

'And were its owners aware of this?'

'Not exactly.'

Guillemot smiled. He didn't like his own islanders, but he disliked the other islanders more. 'So you need help in, shall we say, "fulfilling" your order?'

'Exactly. It might take rather a robust approach.'

Guillemot could see that this could be the chance he'd wished for. That island was rich with things he could trade. And what was more, if he played his cards right he could make some money from this 'Snatcher' in the process.

'So you would like me to provide you with the means to collect what you're after? Perhaps some hired help?'

'Exactly. I think we understand each other very well.'

'And what might you be willing to pay?'

Snatcher liked this man. 'Are you interested in a job?'

'What kind of job?

'One that might be very, very lucrative.'

Guillemot could smell money.

'Once we get what we want we'll be off back to England, but we'll still need more seed. I'll need all I can get, and I need someone here in charge.'

'You're on!'

'So can you provide the help?' Snatcher demanded.

'I think so. It might take a few trinkets. The people around here won't get out of bed unless there is something in it for them.'

# THE SUPERMARKET

Snatcher had a think. 'Is there anything we might offer them?'

'It's really easy. All you have to do is make them want something they don't have. What have you got?'

This baffled Snatcher. He didn't have anything. Was there anything he'd brought with him? Then he remembered . . .

'Do you think they'd like some trotting badgers?'

Guillemot's face dropped. 'Trotting badgers? You've brought trotting badgers halfway around the world?'

'Yes.'

Guillemot thought. If he was on the other island and well out of the way, then he'd rather enjoy the idea of the trotting badgers wreaking havoc on his old 'trading partners'.

'We just have to work out the angle.'

*Guillemot's face dropped*

Once Only Special Offer!

Advance Orders Taken!

Very Limited Supply!

No Cash Needed!

BUY NOW!

PAY LATER!

Chapter 34

# THE HARD SELL

Next morning a very large sign hung over the door of the beach supermarket.

## Once Only Special Offer!

## Advance Orders Taken!

## Very Limited Supply!

## No Cash Needed!

## BUY NOW! PAY LATER!

At nine o'clock, unobserved by anyone, a solitary islander approached the shop, read the sign and disappeared again. Fifteen minutes later, Snatcher, who was waiting inside the

shop with Guillemot and the rest of the crew, heard a sound that at first he couldn't make out. It sounded like a cross between a repeated war cry and a relentless squawking. Then, as the sound got louder and clearer, he smirked. Guillemot's sign had done its job.

'SHOP! SHOP! SHOP! SHOP! SHOP! SHOP! SHOP! SHOP! SHOP! SHOP! SHOP! SHOP!'

Snatcher peered out of the shop door to see the approaching islanders—and got a huge surprise. They were large birds, the size of turkeys, swathed in jewellery and hats, and each carrying a large shopping basket.

*Each carrying a large shopping basket*

'SHOP! SHOP! SHOP! SHOP! SHOP! SHOP! SHOP! SHOP! SHOP! SHOP! SHOP! SHOP!'

The clamouring mass of shopping birds came towards the supermarket.

Gristle spoke. 'Look at 'em all. Loads of them! Do yer think they will be any good in a fight?'

'Not sure,' muttered Snatcher. 'But might be good roasted.'

'SHOP! SHOP! SHOP! SHOP! SHOP! SHOP! SHOP! SHOP! SHOP! SHOP! SHOP! SHOP!'

The birds stopped and fell silent as Guillemot raised a hand.

'As you may have heard I have a very special offer today, and for one day only. A shipment of unequalled value is arriving and it falls to me to offer advance orders. What is more I am not asking for money now . . . or ever!'

The birds started clucking in surprise. It was not what they had come to expect from Guillemot.

'No. What I am asking is for you to sign up to give me just a little help with collection. You'll receive some truly remarkable items and you will be at liberty to do what you want with them. Do I have any takers?'

There was a single squawk of 'YES!' and this set off all the other birds. Guillemot raised his hand again and shouted.

'QUIET! If you want to take advantage of this offer I insist that you form a queue!'

A disorderly queue formed at the gate. There was a lot of pecking as birds tried to outmanoeuvre each other to get closer to the front of the queue.

It only took half an hour to sign them all up, each bird making a beak print on a piece of paper. Snatcher and Gristle were put in charge of this as Guillemot was trying to stop the birds from stealing things from his shelves. This was difficult

as the shop was packed and the birds were taking full advantage. After a while Guillemot just stood at the door and patted down the leaving birds and made them raise their wings. He still lost a lot of stock.

*It only took half an hour to sign them all up*

By eleven, nine hundred birds had signed up and were waiting outside on the beach.

'I think you'd better tell them what they've got to do,' said Guillemot.

'Yes,' smiled Snatcher. 'By the way, Guillemot. Can they fly?'

'No.'

'So how do they get from island to island?'

'Boats. Well, I say boats. More like rafts . . . well actually more like big nests. They use their wings as paddles.'

'Is that how you got across to the other island?'

'Yes. It's not very dignified, but it works. Lost a couple of nests to sharks but I was in the biggest nest and there were no problems.'

*There were no problems*

'Didn't that upset the birds?'

'Not really. Any chance they get to inherit each other's things is seen as positive.'

Snatcher walked outside. He had the measure of the birds.

'Right then. We're off on a little shopping trip.' This was greeted by approving clucking.

'On the other island over there are your new purchases. I'll need a little help getting you your orders.'

'What we got to do?' called out one of the birds.

'It is like this,' explained Snatcher. 'The people on that island might stand in the way when they see what a bargain you're getting. They might put up a fight to stop you getting what's coming to you.'

The birds started squawking in outrage. They liked a fight

but usually only got the chance at the opening of the January sales.

'As you may have noticed we have borrowed their walking monster. We're now going to walk back and I'll need you lot to follow so you can get your bargains. Do you think you can manage that?'

'After the fight do we get our special offer?'

'Oh yes!' smiled Snatcher.

NOCENS SENTENTIA PRO IGNARUS

1 GROAT

# ·THE· Ratbridge·Gazette·

# LONE CHEESE FIEND EVADES CAPTURE

The net is closing as the 'house to house' search continues by day, but by night the fiend is still driven by his evil desires. Police and dogs chased the fiend back into the woods last night after he emerged on what was thought to be yet another of his evil forays. He again escaped down one of the badger tunnels, but not before losing his woolly hat.

In a statement from police it was postulated that this last miscreant had avoided detection by making sure he was free of cheese traces before returning to his lair, thus avoiding detection. But with the woolly hat the police now think they have all they need to trace and forensically link the criminal to the crimes. Large numbers of police are being drafted in from across the county to assist in the sweep of the town and it is thought that by tomorrow night the fiend will be in custody.

The courts of justice have issued a statement that this last and most evil of the 'Cheesy Crims' will receive the heaviest of sentences and that no mercy will be shown.

We here at the Gazette say 'HEAR! HEAR!'

*Suddenly he felt himself pick up speed and rush towards the beach*

## Chapter 35

# THE QUIET BEFORE THE STORM

Arthur was woken by the sun shining on his face. He jumped out of his hammock, feeling totally refreshed after a night in the open air. Smiling, he gazed out towards their ship. It floated calmly in the lagoon and looked at peace.

'I think I will start my day with a swim.' He lifted his clothes over his head, rushed over the sand, and dived in.

Coming up for air, he thought he might try to catch a wave, and body surf in. He had seen some of the island children doing it yesterday and it looked fun. So he swam out a little further. When he saw a wave coming he turned and prepared to catch it. The wave reached him and he paddled as fast as he could. Suddenly he felt himself pick up speed and rush towards the beach. As he did he noticed something was missing.

At first he was not sure what it was, then it struck him. The monster had gone. He wondered if the islanders had moved it. Then he saw Fish come down to the beach. He called out to him.

'Come in and try riding a wave.'

Fish didn't need to be asked twice. As they played, more and more of their friends came to join them in the water. Tom discovered that he could get a very good ride standing on Kipper's stomach and soon all the rats were riding on bellies.

*Tom discovered that he could get a very good ride standing on Kipper's stomach*

The noise didn't take long to wake the islanders. But when the first of them came down they also noticed the lack of monster. Instead of joining the surfers, they ran back to the village to sound the alarm. Arthur and the other surfers saw that something was up and gathered on the beach. Soon the islanders arrived.

'This is bad. It takes quite a few people to operate the monster,' observed Queen Flo.

'And I have a funny feeling I know who they are,' added Bert. 'Shall I go and check?'

'Yes. I think you better had.'

*Bert climbed the rock and looked down the hole*

They all watched as Bert ran across the beach and over to the rocks where the cave was. Bert climbed the rock and looked down the hole. There was the ladder. He signalled a 'thumbs down'.

'I think we have our answer,' said Willbury.

'What do you think that Snatcher is going to do?' asked the Queen.

'Whatever it is, it'll not be good. That you can count on.'

'Where do you think he's gone?'

'The other island. There is nowhere else he could have gone without the ship,' offered Arthur.

'Yup!' said Kipper. 'And he'll be back for the ship and I reckon he might come after the Black Cabbage Seeds as well.'

Bert stood and drew out his sword. 'Well we won't give them to him.'

'Knowing Snatcher he will use any means he can to get what he wants. Are there any weapons on the other island?' asked Arthur.

'No. Just an awful lot of awful birds.'

'What about the shoppers you were telling us about?'

'They are the shoppers.'

'Yes. And how!' answered the Queen as she shook her head.

'Would they help Snatcher?'

'Only if they thought something was in it for them.'

'Well I think we should expect the worst,' said Willbury sadly.

'We can fight Snatcher and his mob . . . and a bunch of birds.' Kipper tried to lift spirits.

'You have to remember that they have our monster, and might have an awful lot of awful big birds, with awful big sharp beaks.'

'What's more we don't know how to fight. We only scare people away,' said the Queen.

'Come on, everyone, we can do it!' said Bert. 'We've been in a fight or two. It's only Snatcher . . . and a bunch of birds . . . and a monster . . . And Snatcher's men, of course . . . How many birds?'

'Could be as many as a thousand.'

Even Bert was silent. Everyone looked at each other in dismay.

Then Marjorie spoke. 'Well, they are going to come if we are ready or not. So it might be better to be as prepared as we can. Any ideas?'

*'How many birds?'*

*Bert was stationed with a telescope in the crow's nest of the ship*

## Chapter 36

# THE BATTLE OF THE BEACH

Everybody mucked in. There was an awful lot to be done if they were to stand any chance of repelling an attack.

To get as early a warning as possible Bert was stationed with a telescope in the crow's nest of the ship. It was agreed that he would signal to the beach as soon as he saw anything.

Arthur was to watch for the signal from Bert, and he was hidden with Fish up a tree on the edge of the beach.

'I hope Snatcher doesn't come back,' he said nervously.

Fish looked gloomy. The prospect of a battle had brought his mood down.

All about below, there were frenetic preparations for what was to come. The pirates and rats searched every corner of the ship for weapons of any sort. Swords, knives, and even wooden spoons were collected and rowed back to the beach. There were not enough to go round so they made spears from bamboo that grew near the beach, clubs from suitable pieces of driftwood, and battleaxes from sticks and anything sharp they could find.

Bert saw that Marjorie was standing on the beach thinking.

'What's up?'

'I think we could handle Snatcher and his mob in a fair fight, but with them having the monster they have the advantage. We have to slow it down or stop it.'

'What should we do?'

'Build defences.'

'Let's get to it then!'

Marjorie told Bert to gather everyone they could including the children and soon homemade shovels and coconut shell 'diggers' were hard at work with sand flying everywhere.

*Soon homemade shovels and coconut shell 'diggers' were hard at work*

After an hour Marjorie said that it might also be very dangerous for the children to be on the beach when the attack came so they were gathered up and led away to safety deep in the jungle.

Once the children had gone a gloom set over the beach and work slowed, until Willbury arrived with some of the villagers who had prepared 'Battle Rations'. This was a very large tray of coconut shells filled with the last of the chocolate from the ship mixed with hot coconut milk and honey. It tasted very good and filled them with new energy as they dug. Soon Marjorie declared the front defences were ready.

'I think they will do. Now it is time to build personal defences and wait.'

'Personal defences?' asked Kipper.

'Yes. You should be good at this. Everybody make themselves a sandcastle big enough to hide behind.'

As the sun grew hotter the beach became dotted with mounds of sand.

*The beach became dotted with mounds of sand*

Kipper, who had proved Marjorie correct about his talents at sandcastle building, had even built an extension to his castle using palm fronds so he could keep in the shade while waiting. This was copied by the others, and as it reached midday it became very quiet on the beach as everyone settled to wait in the shade behind their personal defences.

In the crow's nest Bert was sweltering and very uncomfortable under an umbrella. He was trying to keep his tail in the shade. He'd been hanging it over the side of the barrel in the wind but with the strong sun it had burnt and the skin under the thin hairs was already starting to peel. His mother had warned him about burning his tail but the cool breeze had seemed so tempting.   After tipping a little water from a drinking flask over it he resumed his watch and slowly swung his telescope across the horizon.

*Tipping a little water from a drinking flask*

There it was! It was still a few miles away but the monster was coming. He took a small mirror from his pocket and checked the position of the sun. Then he signalled to Arthur. The sun's beams reflected off the mirror and Bert could see a spot of brighter light on the palm tree below where he knew Arthur was. He moved the mirror and the flash of light flickered over Arthur.

Arthur was startled as the flash of light almost blinded him. Then he realized it was the signal. 'He's seen them. He's seen them. They're coming!'

'Signal back to Bert to let him know you've seen his signal,' called Kipper.

Arthur flashed his mirror back at Bert.

Bert saw the reply and then turned back to watch the approaching attack. He could clearly see the monster and behind it an armada of small boats. As they got closer Bert saw what type of boats they were and what was in the boats.

'My sainted aunt! It's the birds. Blooming loads of them! And in blooming floating nests.'

*'Blooming loads of them!'*

Paddling with wings and simple oars the birds were doing their best to keep up with the mighty monster, but not all of them were faring so well. The swell was having a bad effect on the nest boats and the smaller and more badly built were coming apart and dumping their crew in the sea. Bert noticed that this didn't seem to worry those in the better boats who paddled on without them.

*The swell was having a bad effect on the nest boats*

Bert looked from the weird armada to the beach. Against the monster and the huge number of birds, his friends' preparations looked puny.

'I think they might need my help. Time for a swim!' and with that he launched himself from the crow's nest, plunged down into the sea, and started swimming as fast as he could for the beach.

Arthur watched Bert as he flew from the crow's nest and then swam towards them, then he turned his attention as the others did to the rapidly approaching monster and nest boats. The monster reached the gap in the reef and more of the nests broke up in the surf there, but there were still hundreds of them and even the shipwrecked birds were trailing along behind.

'Stay out of sight and keep quiet!' Marjorie called.

Closer and closer they came. As they reached the shallows the monster rose higher in the water and its legs became visible as it paddled its way towards them. Bert was now only yards ahead in the water and as he reached the sand Kipper broke the silence and called out to him.

'Bert! Over here quick!'

*'Bert! Over here quick!'*

The wet rat ran up the beach and dived behind Kipper's sandcastle.

'I don't know if we are ever going to be able to stop that thing. But I am ready for a fight,' Bert panted.

Then the monster stopped. Arthur saw the glint of metal somewhere on the top of the monster's head. A blade, pushed through from inside, and cutting a flap in the fabric skin. Snatcher's head appeared through the hole, followed by an arm with a megaphone.

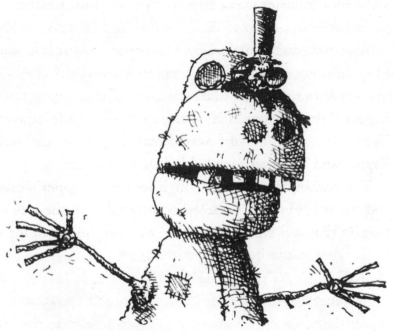

*Snatcher's head appeared followed by an arm with a megaphone*

'Morning! I know you're there, I can sees you from up here. Me and my friends—' at this point he pointed at the mass of floating birds and nest boats that bobbed around him—''ve come to get a few things and if you keep out of our way, there will be no trouble. We might even spare a few lives. But if you don't play along, we is going to give you all a very hard time.'

Kipper and Tom came out from behind their sandcastles. Both had large spears and swords.

'If you don't disappear you will discover you have bitten off more than you can chew,' said Tom bravely.

'That's not the way to speak to a man in control of a sixty-foot monster and a bunch of vicious bird warriors.'

'What!' Kipper scoffed. 'That bunch of turkeys?'

Kipper hadn't quite realized the effect this insult would have on the wet birds. They were furious. No sooner were the words out than the birds started puffing up their chests, flapping their wings and squawking very rude squawks. Even the sound of surf was drowned out by the noise. Kipper and Tom ran back behind their defences.

The combination of the rough journey, Kipper's insult, and the thought that someone was standing in the way of a bargain that was rightfully theirs, was all too much for the birds. They could hold back no longer.

'ATTACK! ATTACK! ATTACK! ATTACK!'

Snatcher had not intended it to go quite this way but there was little he could do about it so he watched as the birds stormed the beach.

The birds leaped ashore and made for the sandcastles where Tom and Kipper were hiding. But as they crossed the high water mark something they were not expecting happened. The birds disappeared.

Marjorie had designed a trap. This consisted of a disguised trench about five feet deep, covered with palm fronds and sand. As soon as the first of the birds realized that they were dropping into a pit they panicked, but this had no effect as the birds behind were so angry that they just charged on. Soon all the birds had disappeared, and the second part of the plan came into action.

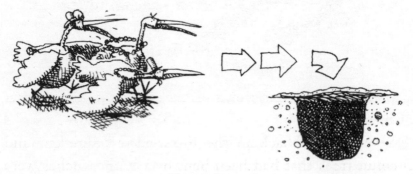

*The trench trap*

'Nets!' shouted Marjorie.

From the cover of the trees, islanders and pirates ran forward pulling nets to seal the birds in. Once the nets were over the trench, rats appeared from holes in the sand and pegged them down.

There was a cheer from Arthur and his friends.

Snatcher watched in disgust.

'Right you lot. You leave me with no choice. I am just going to have to flatten you all.' He looked back down inside the head and bellowed. 'Start the legs and prepare for lunch!'

The monster moved onto the sand and easily stepped right over the trench. Up the tree Arthur could feel the stomp of each footfall.

*The monster moved onto the sand*

'Pull!' shouted Marjorie as she set in motion the next part of their plan.

Several yards back in the forest ropes were cut and coconut trees that had been bent over with winches were released. As the trees sprang up they released coconuts, which flew through the air and hit their target. The monster screamed in several places and looked rather punctured . . .

. . . but still it came on.

*The monster screamed in several places and looked rather punctured*

Marjorie shouted again. 'Operation Lace-up, GO!'

A very long length of rope had been looped around the beach and hidden under the sand. The ends of the rope were being held by two groups of the burliest pirates who, on the command to go, started to pull in the rope. The rope lifted from the sand and caught around the monster's legs.

The monster wavered slightly as the rope pulled tightly round its legs—but then somehow managed to keep moving shakily forwards.

*The rope lifted from the sand and caught around the monster's legs*

'Keep pulling!'

Seeing that the monster seemed unaffected, the islanders ran to join the pirates at each end of the rope. The rope pulled tighter still and for a moment the monster stopped.

Inside, Snatcher was screaming at his crew. 'If yer don't make this thing walk again I will have your guts for garters!'

This seemed to do the trick. The legs strained at the rope and with a loud pop, the rope snapped and the two teams pulling on the ends fell to the ground.

*The two teams pulling on the ends fell to the ground*

'What now?' Kipper shouted to Marjorie.

Marjorie looked distraught. 'I . . . I . . . don't know.'

'We have to do something.'

'Yes, but what?'

Arthur felt Fish pull at his sleeve. The boxtroll wanted to tell him something but didn't have the words. Fish pointed to himself then Arthur, and then to the ground.

'You want me to come with you?'

Fish nodded and quickly shinned down the tree. When they reached the ground Fish looked across at the monster and then to one piece of the broken rope. Then he did something Arthur didn't expect.

Fish ran from the cover of the trees, grabbed the rope and tied a large loop in it. When he'd done this he looked up at the monster. The monster's left foot was about to land only a few feet from the boxtroll.

With enormous courage Fish suddenly threw himself to the ground and rolled right under the foot as it fell. The foot landed ... but Fish had escaped and was now standing on the other side of it. The loop was now around the monster's foot and Fish pulled it tight.

Arthur watched as Fish ran along the beach to the free end of the rope. He picked it up and dived into the waves.

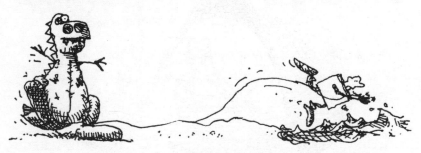

*He picked it up and dived into the waves*

As he did he waved to Arthur to join him. Arthur rushed past the monster and ran into the surf. Fish held the rope high and pointed to the ship.

'I get it! You want us to take the rope out to the ship?'

Fish nodded. Arthur grabbed onto the rope and they began to swim.

Kipper and Tom saw what was happening.

'We need to cause a distraction,' shouted Kipper.

'Got any ideas?'

But before they could come up with anything the monster started to bend over and open its mouth. Kipper looked up and saw something horrid.

'Look! It's got new teeth. Sharp metal ones . . . And they are coming this way.'

The jaws of the monster started to close. Kipper saw it happening and quick as a flash took his thick bamboo spear and forced it between the roof of the monster's mouth and just behind its lower dentures.

*Quick as a flash*

The jaws locked. Tom and Kipper were inside the monster's mouth and could hear Snatcher shouting.

'Raise up the head and chomp them up a bit!'

They rose, but the chomping wasn't working.

'What's going on? Why aren't you chomping them?'

'The jaws are stuck!'

'Apply more pressure!'

Kipper and Tom saw the spear begin to bend.

'It's going to give!'

Tom was holding his spear and pushed it into position alongside the first.

The jaws stopped moving again and there was cursing from somewhere inside the head.

'SONS OF CHEESE THIEVING VERMIN!!!!'

Kipper smiled to Tom. 'He is mad isn't he?'

The spears started to bend.

'More pressure!' screamed Snatcher.

Out in the waves Arthur and Fish heard the twang as the drive belt that drove the jaws broke and the monster's mouth fell open. Kipper and Tom started to fall but as they did Kipper grabbed onto the large cloth tongue with one hand and Tom with the other.

Their friends on the beach held their breath.

'Crawl up my arm!' shouted Kipper as they dangled from the monster's mouth. Tom climbed for all he was worth.

Inside the monster's brain, Snatcher screamed. 'Gristle! Fix those blooming jaws!'

Gristle unbuckled his belt and, as his trousers dropped, managed to tighten it around the cogs that drove the jaws.

Arthur watched, horrified, as the monster's teeth snapped together and a large bump slid down its throat and swelled its belly. But then a sword poked through the wall of the tummy and split to reveal Tom and Kipper, who then jumped to the sand and ran to join their friends, who were so relieved that they let out a cheer.

*A large bump slid down the monster's throat*

'That was close!'

'You are telling me. I thought we had seen the last of you.'

'You should be so lucky.'

Arthur and Fish clambered aboard the ship still clutching the rope.

'What are we going to do?'

Fish waved to Arthur to follow him. The boxtroll fed the rope around one of the winches and fixed it.

'You are going to wind him in?'

*They both grabbed the spars of the winch and started to push*

Fish smiled. They both grabbed the spars of the winch and started to push. Quickly the slack in the rope wound in. Then almost as soon as the rope was tight a gentle breeze came up from the west and started to push against the ship. This tightened the rope even more and began to pull on the monster's leg.

'What's happening? I didn't tell you to turn this thing around,' snapped Snatcher to Gristle.

'I ain't doing nothing!'

'Well how come we is turning round?'

'I'm not sure. Why don't you have a look upstairs?' Gristle pointed at the hole in the top of the monster's head.

Snatcher looked out.

'OH MY GAWD! They got us tied to the ship and is pulling us out.'

'What do you want us to do?'

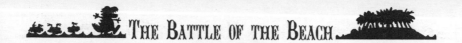

Snatcher could see that if he resisted the ship and the rope didn't snap they would be pulled over.

'Turn out to sea and start walking!'

There was renewed cheering as the monster retreated back into the sea.

'Well done, Arthur and Fish!'

Snatcher was reassessing the situation.

'OK then. I get to control the ship and by the look of it I might get a couple of hostages out of it this way. Not so bad. I might enjoy a little punishing of hostages!'

He looked down inside the head.

'Right, lads! I think I've just sorted things. Make ready for boarding.'

*The monster retreated back into the sea*

NOGENS SENTENTIA PRO IGNARUS

1 GROAT

# THE ·Ratbridge·Gazette·

# LATE EXTRA

## Mass Breakout Of Cheese Crims Causes Panic!

While police were conducting their sweep of the whole town in the search for the last cheese fiend, the other 'Cheese Crims' housed at Ratbridge gaol rioted, smashed down the gates, escaped and are even now causing panic across the town. The mob seems to be moving towards the cheese marshes in an attempt to satisfy their lust.

Lock yourselves in your homes until the mob is quelled!

*The monster loomed towards the ship*

Chapter 37

# UNDER NEW MANAGEMENT

The monster loomed towards the ship and as it did Arthur and Fish went from feelings of triumph to fear of what would happen when the monster arrived.

'What are we going to do?' exclaimed Arthur.

Fish looked worried and clueless.

'I don't think we will be able to defend the ship so I think we better swim for it! Over the side!'

They both climbed on the rail, jumped, and swam wide of the monster and headed for the beach. As they swam, Arthur looked back and saw Snatcher and his men climbing from the head of the monster and jumping down onto the ship.

*They both swam wide of the monster and headed for the beach*

'I am not sure that was such a good idea,' he called over to Fish, suddenly realizing that they might have made things even worse.

Despite this they were met with cheers as they reached the beach.

'Well done Fish, and Arthur!' called out Willbury. 'You've saved us!'

'I am not sure that we have really helped. Snatcher has taken control of the ship,' replied Arthur.

*'Snatcher has taken control of the ship!'*

A solemn silence fell over the beach. As they gazed out across the water they could just make out the forms of Snatcher and his mob standing on deck and they seemed to be laughing.

'Now what?' asked Kipper.

On board, Snatcher started dishing out orders.

'Strip down the monster and stow it. I think it will be very useful when we get back to Blighty. And Gristle . . . get me some paper and a quill.'

Gristle lowered himself over the stern to the captain's cabin, then returned back up the rope.

'The smell down there is awful. I think one of the trotting badgers must have food poisoning.'

'Ah yes, the dear trotting badgers. I'll have to include them in the deal.'

'What deal?'

'Well, we have the ship and if our friends want to get home they will have to do exactly what I tell them. This is going to be fun.'

*'If our friends want to get home they will have to do exactly what I tell them'*

For the next hour or so, Snatcher sat writing and rewriting a letter of terms. When it was done he was looking very pleased with himself and chuckled as he poked the letter into a bottle and pushed in a cork.

'Gristle. Swim ashore and parley with them blighters.'

'What, me?'

'Yes, you!'

Gristle could see that there was no way of getting out of it.

'What do you want me to say?'

'Nothing. Just give 'em the bottle and wait for the reply. It is going to be a joy to behold.'

*'This is outrageous!'*

## Chapter 38

# DEAL OR NO DEAL

'This is outrageous!' Willbury snorted after briefly inspecting the letter Gristle had just handed him.

Gristle didn't know quite how to react. His boss had the upper hand, but here he was at the mercy of the enemy. He decided it was best to look at what remained of his old boots.

'What does Snatcher say?' asked Tom.

'Quite a lot. And most of it unrepeatable.'

'Is it some kind of deal?'

'For him it is. I'll read it out . . . apart from the rude bits at the beginning, and end . . . and a few bits in the middle.'

'Let's hear it then,' sighed Marjorie.

'Dear bunch of misfits, failed lawyers, pathetic pirates, filthy rats, and other assorted losers, if you ever wish to see England again you'll follow the following instructions to the letter. Please deliver to the ship the following:

'One: Enough food and water for the journey home. It won't be necessary to provide much for any of you lot who want to come with us, as prisoners will be on quarter rations. Provisions will include at least ten cheeses from the forest and as much fuel as can be gathered and stowed.

'Two: One ton of Black Cabbage seed.'

'What does he want that lot for? It takes less than one seed to poison someone.' Queen Flo was outraged.

Willbury shook his head. 'I think there's no helping the man.'

'Or most of England if he gets hold of that stuff,' added Arthur.

Willbury continued reading.

'Three: Signed statements from everybody wishing to return to England, admitting mutiny.'

'If we agreed to that we could all end up in prison or transported,' scoffed Bert.

*'in prison or transported'*

'I know, but if we're to get back we might just have to take our chance. I doubt very much if Snatcher is going to want to have a lot to do with the legal system back home, but it would be a huge risk.' Willbury did not look happy, but went on.

'In addition to the above, agreement to the following:

'Four: That everybody who wishes to travel home will submit to a search, to make sure they are not carrying any Un-Cabbage Flowers or weapons.

'Five: That all prisoners will sign another undertaking not to mention any details of this trip to anyone, and failure to do so will lead to loss of all personal possessions.

'Six: This contract will stand under the statutes of English, International, and Island law.'

'So if we sign we get to go home, but heaven knows what will happen when we get there?' said Marjorie.

'You never know what Snatcher might have got planned for us on the way home, either. Once we are on the ship we would be at his mercy,' added Bert.

'Why don't we just wait until the next ship comes along?' asked Kipper.

'We could do, but if we stay here we have no idea when we might get home, and what we'll find when we get there,' said Willbury. 'With all those cabbage seeds Snatcher could cause untold mayhem.'

'And if he takes that monster back too, he'll be unstoppable,' Bert added.

'And I need to get back to Grandfather!' said Arthur urgently. 'I can't leave him alone, especially if Snatcher is going back to cause more trouble.'

'Anyway,' said Marjorie firmly, 'we can't do what he asks. There's just no way we can hand over wild cheeses, or the cabbage seeds.'

'If you want to go home you's going to have to accept the lot,' Gristle muttered.

Queen Flo spoke again. 'We haven't actually seen any wild cheeses for at least two years. Tell Snatcher if he wants the cheeses he might have to wait a long, long time.'

Gristle looked worried. 'He ain't goin' to like that.'

'Would you mind leaving us alone for a few minutes?'

Gristle wandered off to poke the trapped shopping birds with a stick while the terms were discussed.

*Gristle wandered off to poke the trapped shopping birds with a stick*

'So what do we do?'

Arthur felt awful. 'I have to go back. How can I stay here not knowing what's happening to Grandfather? Perhaps Snatcher will agree to take just me without the cheeses and the cabbage seeds.'

'If one of us goes back, we all have to,' Willbury said solemnly.

'Willbury is right,' said Bert. 'I think we will have to accept Snatcher's conditions and take our chance. There is no way Arthur can stay here while his grandfather is ill, and we all have to do our best to stop Snatcher getting loose with that monster back home.'

It seemed very sad but they'd have to aid Snatcher—at least for now.

'Then we will just have to come up with a plan to make sure we can get the better of Snatcher and his men,' said Marjorie.

'Like what?'

'I'm not sure yet, but it had better be good.'

*'Like what?'*

*The birds were extremely unhappy*

## Chapter 39

# PROVISIONS

The next two days were frenetic. The first job was releasing the shopping birds. The birds were extremely unhappy. Surprisingly not so much at being trapped, but at not getting the bargain deal they'd signed up for. Bert took charge of proceedings and ordered his helpers to arm themselves with their spears—but to wrap towels around one end so as not to puncture the birds. Then, while one group held down the birds with their padded spears, others released the pegs. As soon as the net was off the birds struggled so much that it became impossible to restrain them, and Bert's crew pulled back to avoid being pecked. The birds jumped out of the pit. Then they started complaining about not getting their special deal. Bert was not sure what to do and as the threat of pecking seem to have passed he guessed it would be all right just to let them wander about until hopefully they

would find their way home. This didn't happen. Instead the birds got in the way of everything, and filled the air with complaints. Kipper was very tempted to insult them again when two birds started following him and telling him that if they didn't get their deal they would go to see the local trading standards officer and possibly write to the paper. Fortunately Tom stopped him in time.

'Apart from frying them, what are we going to do with them?' whispered Kipper.

'I'm not sure. They just won't stop going on about this blooming deal that Snatcher promised them,' Tom replied. 'But we've got to do something—I don't think I can stand much more of this squawking.'

'It's obvious that Snatcher offered them some sort of deal to get them to help him. He probably never intended to carry it through. Perhaps we should ask him about it. Something has to be done otherwise we are never going to get the provisions he wants onboard.'

'You are right. If he want the provisions he has to get the birds off our backs.'

Kipper and Tom took one of the fishing boats and rowed out to the ship and asked to speak to Snatcher. They waited for a minute or two then Snatcher came to the rail and eyed them up.

'What do you two want?'

'The shopping birds are causing problems with us getting your provisions ready. Since we released them, all they have done is wander about complaining about some deal you made with them and getting in the way. It's making it almost impossible to work. We wonder if you might be able to sort the situation out.'

*'What do you two want?'*

Snatcher smiled slyly.

'Don't worry. I can sort this. Can't have them disturbing the provisions. Just row back and tell them that they will be given everything they were promised as a big thank you for helping me out. Then use the boats to ferry them out here and we'll use the ship to take them back to their island and give them what they have got coming.'

When Kipper and Tom returned to the beach the birds were delighted with the news and without any instruction formed an excited queue at the water's edge. The complaints were now replaced with feverish speculation as to what they were about to receive, and delight at not having to travel back to their island in the nest boats.

'What do you think Snatcher is going to give them?' Arthur asked Tom.

'Whatever it is I am sure it's no real bargain.'

Quiet returned to the beach as the birds departed, and once they were aboard, the ship set off to their island. A few hours later the ship returned with only Snatcher and his crew.

On the beach the provisions stacked up and the fishing boats started to ferry them across to the ship. Arthur was aboard one of the first loads and noticed a couple of rather strange changes. The crew looked a little battered and had lots of fresh cuts and bruises, and the doors down to the Captain's cabin were open again. Gristle and some of the others were washing down the stairwell.

Gristle noticed him looking at them. 'We got rid of them badgers as well.'

This seemed a bit odd but even Arthur sighed with relief at the idea of not having to share the journey home with them.

(Little did Arthur know but only six weeks later the shopping birds would become extinct, and a few months after that, a whaling ship found a man floating in an open boat in the middle of the Pacific. The man was covered in scars and asked his rescuers if they would like to buy a vest.)

The list of provisions was ticked off as it was loaded from the beach and finally all that was left was the black cabbage seeds. There were very mixed feelings about handing these over but little else could be done if Arthur and his friends were ever to get home. The villagers had gathered sacks of seeds from the forest and there was a very ominous feeling when it became time to load them onto the boats.

Willbury watched as the heavy sacks were placed in the boats, then turned and shook his head.

With everything needed for the voyage on board, Snatcher announced they were to leave the following morning. On shore for the last night the islanders gave the prisoners a last feast. Things seemed not to have turned out well but the islanders gave their new friends as much of a party as the mood allowed. A pit was dug and large rocks taken from a fire were placed in it and then parcels of food wrapped in banana leaves were placed on the rock before the pit was filled with sand and allowed to bake for a few hours. When the food was served Arthur and his friends declared that it really was some of the best food they had ever eaten. They drank coconut shell after coconut shell of fruit juices and took it in turns to sing songs. The rats and pirates sang sea shanties and the islanders sang their own local lullabies. The singing went on long into the night, but slowly they settled in their hammocks amongst the trees for the last time.

Arthur lay looking up at the stars. It felt very strange.

Here he was in such a beautiful place, but tomorrow he and his friends were going to give themselves up to Snatcher. It was the early hours before he finally went to sleep.

At daybreak he awoke and found his friends around him, taking down their hammocks and packing up their things in silence. They finished a breakfast of fresh fruit as they knew it would be a long time till they ate so well again and then loaded up fishing boats while the islanders chatted to them and looked on. As they climbed aboard there were many hugs and quite a few tears.

Then Queen Flo spoke. 'We wish we could have met you in different circumstances, but we wish you well and hope that an opportunity to turn things around comes up.'

'We really must thank you,' replied Willbury. 'I think you know we'll be looking for every chance that comes along.'

*They were searched right down to their underpants*

With that the boats set off from the shore towards the ship. When they reached the ship one 'prisoner' was allowed on deck at a time, and as they were they were searched right down to their underpants to make sure that no Un-Cabbage Flowers were being hidden. The gloom on the faces of the prisoners seemed to delight Snatcher's men and they took great pleasure in poking fun at them and telling them how they would punish them if the prisoners stepped out of line. Even Bert held his tongue when Gristle made jokes about his red tail.

The fishing boats went back to the beach and the islanders returned to wave a last farewell as the anchor was raised. Arthur and his friends were sad to be leaving their island and—between the many jobs they were given— waved until the ship was long past the reef and the island was almost lost from sight.

'I am sorry we brought trouble to them,' said Arthur.

'Yes. They didn't deserve it. Perhaps they can get back to the quiet life now,' replied Willbury as he watched the disappearing island.

'I doubt it will be as quiet a life now that their monster has been taken away. Anybody might turn up.'

So the return journey began and Snatcher was revelling in his power. He was very, very careful to keep the guard on the prisoners and would have happily locked them below but he knew that his 'officers' were incapable of sailing the ship home.

'It won't stop me dropping them in the drink when we get close to home though,' he confided to Gristle. 'And the Good Doctor and Fingle might be going for a dip as well . . . '

*'It won't stop me dropping them in the drink'*

The ship sailed south and things got a lot rougher, both the sea, and the prisoners' treatment at the hands of the 'officers'. In the bilges it was foul, wet, and the hammocks swung so violently that it was almost impossible to sleep, so Arthur and most of his friends spent as much time on deck as possible. Only Fish seemed to revel in the high seas. He had become a true sailor.

As Arthur helped Kipper at the helm they watched Fish standing at the rail on the forecastle being washed with the spray from the waves.

'He's changed so much. It is hard to imagine any other boxtroll taking to the seas like he has,' Kipper said admiringly.

'He looks in his element. Almost as much as any of you pirates.'

'Yes. The first boxtroll pirate, and a fine one.'

'I'm not sure I'm cut out to be a pirate.'

'You're not doing too badly. There is many a man that would be proud to be able to take seas like this as well as you.' And Kipper winked at him and pointed to a couple of Snatcher's men who were looking very green.

Then in a very loud voice Kipper asked Arthur, 'Do you fancy something to eat. I could murder a bacon sandwich with lots of grease and butter.'

'Yes,' smiled Arthur. 'Followed up with a plateful of sausages and more bread dipped in dripping.'

Their guards seemed to have been affected badly by the talk of food and were now 'being ill' over the rail.

'I don't like the look of the sea you know. I think it is only just starting to get rough. Fancy a plate of fried eggs and ham?'

'Not half! And washed down with a pint of raw eggs.'

Arthur and Kipper smiled but stopped torturing their guards at this point because they were being so ill that it was a distinct possibility that one of them might fall over the side.

As they reached the Cape the sea did indeed become rougher and all but the hardest of sailors and Fish went off

their food. Arthur was feeling so sick he just hung in the dark in his swaying hammock in the bilges, moaned and thought about home.

'How I wish I was back in Ratbridge,' he muttered.

'Me too!' came a weak reply from Willbury who was also too ill to go on deck.

'Do you think we will ever get there?'

'I am not sure I won't die first,' came another voice. It was a weakly moaning Marjorie.

'We are not going to die. Just think of the job we have to do and how we have to save your grandfather and the others,' came Willbury's voice from the dark again.

Arthur had indeed been trying to think of his grandfather and how he was getting on, but it was hard to concentrate with feeling so ill.

'I think I'd take the jollop if it made me feel better than this.'

*There was also a terrible smell from rotting seaweed*

# Chapter 40

# THE DOLDRUMS

For five days the weather was terrible but on the day of the sixth the sea became calmer and the sickness subsided. The ship had turned north into the Atlantic, and now with every day they sailed it became warmer again. The ship started making good time, but then they reached the doldrums.

Just east of Brazil the wind completely died away. The water became glassy, the air very hot, and very still. With the monster and all the seeds they'd packed there had not been as much space for fuel and little was left.

'What do we do, captain?' asked Kipper.

Snatcher didn't like this heat. It felt damp. There was also a terrible smell from rotting seaweed that floated all around them.

'Burn everything that we don't need.'

'What don't we need?'

Snatcher had to think. There was almost nothing they didn't need on board if he wanted to have a monster and still be able to go through with his plan for free black jollop for all of England.

'Burn the furniture!' he ordered.

This took about a day before it was gone.

'What next?' asked Kipper.

'Burn the ship's biscuits.'

This only kept them going for three hours.

'And now, there's nothing left but your monster and the seeds?'

Snatcher's skin was coming up in heat bumps and he was sweaty and itching very badly.

'If I burn the seeds I ain't going to be able to make more poison, but if I burn the monster I won't be able to induce terror . . . This is a tricky one.' He stuck a hopeful finger in the air to see if he could feel any breeze, but all be could feel was the sun beating down on his exposed spotty red forearm.

'If we burnt a bit of the monster we might just keep going until the wind picks up,' suggested Gristle.

The over-hot and bothered Snatcher clomped Gristle around the head with the umbrella he was using as a sunshade.

'Don't be stupid. Who is going to be afraid of an almost complete monster?'

'Well, what we going to do? We could just fade away if we stay here.'

Snatcher looked from his heat bumps to the sacks of seeds.

'Maybe if we burnt just some of the seeds until the wind picked up . . . ' Making up his mind suddenly, he turned to Kipper. 'Burn five sacks of the seeds. But mind, only five sacks, and we will see where that gets us.'

Kipper smiled. A few minutes later the first of the sacks was opened and spadefuls of the seeds were shovelled into the boiler.

The fire started to roar and a thick black disgustingly smelly smoke poured out of the chimney, and the ship started to make headway again. By the time the fourth sack was burnt a change had come over everyone. Even Snatcher's heat bumps had miraculously disappeared and he was feeling very perky.

'Right! Back to Ratbridge . . . and quickly. I am feeling very peckish,' ordered Snatcher.

Marjorie sneaked up to Willbury and whispered to him. 'Do you realize what has happened?'

*'Do you realize what has happened?'*

'No. But I do feel oddly rather good. And there is something else. I keep thinking of my childhood . . . sitting in front of the fire eating something.' Then a look of guilty horror crossed his face. 'Slices of . . . no . . . no . . . cheese on toast!'

'It's the fumes from the seeds. It's got into us all and though it might be making us feel better it will also be poisoning us with the cheese lust.'

'What do we do?'

'I think there is only one thing we can do.'

Marjorie fetched Fish from the bow and took him down to the bilges. Then she sent for Arthur.

'I want you to bring down each of our crew and friends. Only let a few down at a time and make sure that it's not noticed.'

'Aye, aye!'

'And before you go have this.'

In the darkness of the bilges Arthur saw a large blue glowing bottle appear from under Fish's box.

*A large blue glowing bottle*

'You got some on board!'

'Yes. Snatcher's mob have such contempt for boxtrolls we knew they wouldn't search him. Now open your mouth.'

Marjorie gave him a few drops of its contents on a spoon.

'It tastes like violets.'

As the taste spread over his tongue he felt a tingling in his body and the odd craving that had been occupying Arthur's mind seemed to just slip away.

'Now go and tell the others to get down here.'

Small groups of his friends disappeared below deck and returned looking happier.

As the last of the five sacks went in the boiler Kipper asked Snatcher what to do.

'Burn another sack! We need to go faster. And by the way, would it be just as quick to get to somewhere like Camembert in France as Ratbridge?'

'No, Camembert is inland.'

'Well, just get on with the stoking and head for England.'

'And when we finish that sack?'

'Burn some more! Just get us back to Ratbridge as fast as you can.'

Kipper smiled to himself. Snatcher had been given his own medicine and now didn't care if all the seeds got burnt.

'Stoke the boilers and full steam ahead!'

It took only a few more sacks until they were clear of the doldrums, but Snatcher ordered more seeds to be burnt. He and his mob were so infected with the fumes of the seeds that cheese plagued their every waking moment. All that drove them now was the idea of cheese and the only place they could think that they could get hold of some was the woods around Ratbridge.

Fish moved to the stern deck with Kipper because Snatcher wanted to be closer to home and took the place on the bow.

Then as the last sack became empty they reached home waters.

Snatcher came aft and spoke. 'I want you to anchor off Weston-super-mare. It's a town down the coast from Bristol.'

'I know it,' said Kipper. 'My mum used to drag me there when I was a kid. Why do you want to stop there?'

'Never you mind. Just get us there.'

As the sun rose the following morning the anchor was dropped. They were about a mile from the coast but the water was very shallow.

Snatcher ordered his men to lock the crew below. 'We don't want any interference while we get on with me plan.'

Arthur and the others sat in their hammocks.

'What is he up to?'

'No good I'm sure but at least he's not got any seeds left.'

Then there was a bump and the ship became still.

'What's happened?'

'The tide must have gone out. We must be on the sand.'

There seemed to be a lot of activity above them and then

it went quiet. After a few more hours the ship seemed to be floating again but apart from the sound of water there was little other noise.

'What do we do now?'

'I think they have deserted us. It's probably the time to escape from here.'

'How do we do that?'

Fish took a crowbar from under his box and handed it to Kipper. Kipper pushed the end of it into the crack at the edge of the hatch and pushed.

There was a crack and the hatch popped open. Everyone rushed up on deck. Willbury was right. Snatcher and his men had gone . . . and so had all the bits of the monster.

*Fish took a crowbar from under his box*

*'Attack of the seventy-foot monster! Read all about it!'*

## Chapter 41

# BRISTOL

With Snatcher and his men out of the way, and a following wind, it only took a few hours for the ship to reach Bristol. A pilot came out to meet them and guide them back up the river. As they came to the dock they put in to buy some coal for the boiler as there was now almost nothing onboard left to burn. As they tied up Arthur heard a boy crying out:

'*Evening Post, Evening Post!* Read all about it. Attack of the seventy-foot monster! Read all about it!'

Arthur rushed down the gangplank, bought a paper, and started to read.

### 'SOMERSET VILLAGE ATTACKED BY HUGE MONSTER!

```
This afternoon word arrived that
the village of Cheddar was attacked
```

by a seventy-foot tall monster. The
village is the last resting home of
the cave-dwelling Cheddar cheeses,
and these seemed to be the target.
As the monster attacked and tried
to gain entrance to the caves, the
cheeses made off down the tunnels
deep into the bowels of the earth.
Denied its quarry, the monster made
off in a north-easterly direction.
Unconfirmed sightings of the
monster were also made at Weston.
Witnesses claim the monster emerged
from the sea at low tide.'

Arthur finished reading and ran back onto the ship.

'Quick. Snatcher is on the rampage. We have to get back to Ratbridge.'

Quickly they cast off again and headed up river towards the canal. Tom and Bert took up position up in the crow's nest with the telescope and scanned the countryside for any signs of a monster.

*Tom and Bert took up position up in the crow's nest*

Arthur stood on the bow with Fish and, when they reached the canal, helped operate the lock gates. It was another half an hour before there was a cry from Bert.

'There she blows! Monster at twenty-five degrees to port.' They all looked out over the port bow.

Over the tops of some trees in the distance they saw the shape of the monster's head.

'It's heading for Ratbridge!' shouted Bert.

*They saw the shape of the monster's head*

*'IT'S A BLOOMING MONSTER AND IT'S COMING THIS WAY!'*

## Chapter 42

# CHEEZILLA!

The Ratbridge police now spent every afternoon patrolling the town walls and keeping an eye out for cheese-crazed inhabitants planning a break to satisfy their lust. If they'd only needed to guard the gates it would have been easy but now the cheese-crazed inhabitants had taken to using ropes and ladders to escape over the walls as the sun set in a desperate attempt to get to the woods to hunt the remaining cheeses.

Constable Grunt was brewing up tea for his patrol and emptying the last brew's tea leaves over the wall when he happened to look across to the wood. In the distance over the trees he could vaguely make out something moving.

'What do you reckon that is?' he asked a fellow officer.

'Not sure. Maybe . . .' His friend scratched his head and looked perplexed. 'I don't know.'

'It seems to be getting bigger.'

'Or closer?'

'What shall we do?'

'Eeeer . . . Blow your whistle?'

Grunt did as suggested and from along the wall the police came to see what was up. Soon they all stood watching the 'thing' moving through the trees.

Inside the wall those with the craving who were watching the police for a chance to escape from the town started to climb the unguarded parts of the wall. Ladders appeared and bodies could soon be seen mounting the wall and dropping ropes over the outside. But before anyone had managed to actually escape one of the policemen who had better sight than the others spoke.

'It's a blooming monster.'

'A what!'

'IT'S A BLOOMING MONSTER AND IT'S COMING THIS WAY!'

'My Gud! What about them what's guarding the swamp. It's nearly out of the woods and then it will be on them!'

'Everybody blow your whistle to warn them!'

As the monster broke from the woods the policemen surrounding the swamp heard the noise from the town walls and then turned to see the huge creature. They did what was natural and ran away screaming.

Across the town word travelled that there was something coming and people flocked to the walls to get a look. But as they crammed the walls they saw how huge and dangerous it looked and everybody started to scream.

The ship, fuelled with coal, made fast progress up the canal and was in clear sight of the town when the monster broke from the woods.

'Stop the engine!' Bert cried from the crow's nest.

Everyone aboard rushed to the rail to watch as the mighty beast began lurching towards the nearby swamp.

'What's he going to do now?' Kipper asked.

'Heaven knows, with Snatcher crazed with the cheese lust,' answered Willbury.

'I reckon he'll try to snap up any last remaining cheeses and then turn on the town,' said Bert.

'So what do we do?' asked Kipper. Everybody thought hard but it was Arthur that spoke first.

'Use his cheese lust,' suggested Arthur tentatively.

'What do you mean?' asked Kipper.

'Well, he wants cheese desperately and we need to slip him some of the antidote before he devours the last of the cheese or destroys the town while he's crazed. Can't we combine the two?'

'But how?'

'Make a fake cheese filled with the antidote.'

Kipper smiled. 'I get it. We bamboozle him with a cheese. But how do we get it in front of him?'

'Cheeses have legs don't they? One of us is inside the cheese,' offered Arthur.

'But wouldn't that be putting whoever is inside the cheese in terrible danger?'

'We make sure they have an escape,' Arthur replied. 'And choose the fastest runner to be the cheese.'

'But how do we make a cheese?'

Arthur looked thoughtful. 'For the smell socks might work. Have you never noticed the pong that dirty ones make?'

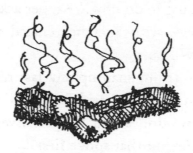

*'For the smell socks might work'*

'And boy do we ever have some dirty socks,' said Kipper enthusiastically.

'I reckon I could mould a cheesy body with sock smell and the antidote pretty easily in the galley,' Bert offered.

'Well then. It might just work,' chuckled Tom.

'Great. But who's the fastest runner?' asked Marjorie.

'Us rats are pretty fast,' Tom boasted.

'Not that fast really. Your legs are pretty short. I think in an open space a human could run faster,' replied Kipper.

'I'll do it,' said Arthur. 'I can run fast and it was my idea.'

Willbury looked very concerned. 'It is too dangerous. There is a real danger of being eaten. Besides, your legs are not that long.'

'And imagine what the smell would be like,' added Bert. 'It might make you pass out.'

'Anybody got a better idea?' asked Arthur.

No one had.

Arthur looked about. 'Well then, we have to do something and fast. It may be our only way to save the real cheeses and Ratbridge.'

'Arthur is right. So how do we choose who is going to be our cheese?' asked Kipper.

'A race. We could have a race up the deck,' suggested Bert.

Willbury looked at Arthur. 'I really don't want you involved in this.'

Arthur smiled back. 'This is about who is fastest and can do the job best. It has to be the fastest runner. Anyway, I think you need to give me a chance to be useful. Remember that you didn't want me to come on this voyage at all. Where would you all be now if I hadn't stowed away?'

'That's true. But hopefully you won't win.'

'A race from one end of the deck to the other it is then,' said Bert.

Even though it was going to be a very dangerous mission, everyone crowded to the fore end of the deck and Willbury set them off with a count of three.

By the time Arthur had reached halfway along the deck Fish was in the lead, just a few paces ahead.

'I know I can do this,' Arthur thought to himself as he pushed himself as hard as he could and began to catch up with the boxtroll.

*Fish was in the lead*

He gritted his teeth and pumped his legs as hard as he could, then as the side of the ship came closer he reached out with his hand and stretched.

'ARTHUR'S WON!'

His friends crowded around him. They looked pleased for him—but very concerned too.

'Well done! But I'll go if you don't want to,' offered Kipper.

'I think that would be best,' said Willbury—but then he bowed his head in resignation as Arthur looked him in the eye and spoke very firmly.

'I am the fastest and I think that I can do the job. Let's get ready. Time to make our cheese substitute!'

Bert quickly took charge of making the 'cheese'. First he got everybody to put every dirty sock they could find in the biggest saucepan they had. He added water, then after a good stir he strained off the liquid into another pan and added flour and some yellow ointment that they used to rub on scuffed knees.

'And of course our secret ingredient!'

Fish reached inside his box and pulled out the glowing blue bottle. Bert took it and tipped its contents into the mixture. After a bit of a stir it became much thicker and looked like bright yellow dough.

*Bert took it and tipped its contents into the mixture*

'Still a bit soggy. How are we going to get it to stick to Arthur?'

'I have some glue that goes hard after ten minutes. We could mix that in?' suggested Marjorie.

'Very well. We'll use that. If we cut two holes in the bottom of a barrel we can put Arthur's legs through them and use it as a mould. Arthur, strip down to your underpants, then we will cover you in grease.'

While Marjorie fetched the quick setting glue, Arthur was readied and two holes were cut in the bottom of a barrel.

Then Arthur was lowered into the barrel, leaving him with his legs sticking out of the bottom and his head out of the top.

The reality of the situation began to dawn on Arthur. Yes, he had won the race, but would he really be fast enough to outrun the monster? Maybe Willbury was right—maybe he really *would* get eaten . . . But it was too late for doubts now.

'Are you ready?' Bert asked.

'Ready as I'll ever be.'

The glue was tipped into the dough mixture and stirred in.

'You'd better be quick or it will go hard in the pan.'

'OK!'

*The foul-smelling mixture was tipped into the barrel around Arthur*

The foul-smelling mixture was tipped into the barrel around Arthur. It felt warm around his belly as the mixture hardened. After a couple of minutes the mixture stiffened and Bert declared it ready.

'Take the barrel apart!' Bert instructed and the metal hoops were knocked loose and slid off. The barrel fell apart leaving Arthur standing on the deck looking like . . . an enormous cheese.

*Arthur looking like an enormous cheese*

'Perfect! Not only does he look like a cheese but he also smells like one.'

Arthur's arms were free above his new cheese body so he was able to hold his nose.

'So what happens now?' asked Willbury in a worried tone.

'Arthur lures the monster away from the real cheeses in the woods,' replied Bert

'But where to?' Willbury seemed increasingly worried.

'If we dig a hole in the ground I could slip out of the costume into it,' suggested Arthur.

'I guess we need to dig the hole then?' said Kipper.

'Where?' Willbury was starting to panic. 'This really is not a good idea.'

'Don't worry. Somewhere between the woods and the town so he doesn't have to run too far,' answered Kipper. 'Our Arthur can do it!'

The sound of roaring rang out from the woods.

'We'd better be quick! Grab a spade, Tom, and come with me,' shouted Kipper.

The pirates jumped over the side and ran to a place not far from the town wall. There they quickly dug a hole a little taller than Arthur and just wide enough for his body.

*They quickly dug a hole*

Arthur watched from the deck of the ship. He had been wrapped in oilskin to stop the smell getting out too early. They didn't want anything to happen before they were ready.

Bert and Fish stood next to him.

'What do you think I should do to attract them?'

'I think you won't have to worry too much. And we'll

help. You'll just have to run about a bit like a cheese until they get close.'

Kipper and Tom returned.

'Are you ready?'

'Yes,' said a nervous Arthur.

'You don't have to do this! You can still back out.' Willbury was looking very pale and Marjorie led him away from the crowd.

Arthur looked about for a moment, with a worried expression on his face. Kipper put a hand on his shoulder.

'He's right. You don't have to do this.'

'No. I want to do it.'

'Good lad!'

The gangplank was lowered to the canal bank, and Arthur smiled at Kipper and his friends. 'Well, let's go then!'

*'Are you ready?'*

*Arthur stood waiting a few yards from the hole*

## Chapter 43

# A Cheesy Ending

Arthur stood waiting a few yards from the hole. It seemed pointless and a bit embarrassing to start running about before anybody saw him, so he waited for the others to do their work.

Half the crew went into the town. The other half headed towards the monster.

Then it began.

'Cheese! Cheese! A huge wild cheese!' All over town the cry rang out. Heads popped out of windows.

*Heads popped out of windows*

'Where's the cheese? Where's the cheese?'

'Just outside the town wall. It's huge!'

The pirates' cries were soon mixed with the sound of running footsteps.

Across the fields the rest of the crew were in sight of the monster.

'Cheese! Cheese! Cheese!' they shouted as they waved their arms to get noticed.

Inside the head of the monster Snatcher's ears heard the cry.

'Who's shouting that?'

'I don't know but it's coming from outside.'

'It must be a trap. Why else would anybody be shouting cheese?'

The eyes of the monsters turned to the shouting crew, who then pointed towards a small shape just outside the town walls. The monster looked up and saw the shape.

'It looks like a cheese, boss!'

The nose then reported back. 'I can smell it. Ripe smelly cheese.'

'Don't seem quite right. Hold on, boys!'

The thought of cheese was too much for his mob. No way were they going to hang about if there was a chance of eating cheese.

'Legs full ahead! Let's get some cheese,' screamed Gristle.

'No! NO!' shouted Snatcher. 'It's probably a trap.' But even he was salivating.

Arthur was getting worried as he saw the monster turn towards him. He spun round towards the town and was about to start running in that direction when a mob started to pour from the town gate.

'CHEESE! CHEESE! IT'S A CHEESE!'

He was not sure which way to turn.

'Stay calm! I have to stay calm . . . and act like a cheese.'

He decided to run in circles around the hole. If he did that he could get to it at any moment.

*He decided to run in circles around the hole*

The monster and the mob grew closer. Arthur thought it looked as if the monster would reach him first. He was not sure this was a good thing. It might scare off the mob, so he stopped and waggled his cheese body at the mob.

The cries of 'CHEESE' grew louder.

Arthur turned to check and was horrified. Powered by the lust for cheese the monster was striding rapidly towards him, much faster than he had imagined. It was almost time to run . . . NO! He mustn't run. He just had to jump in the hole.

The urge to turn and run was huge but he resisted it. So he stood right over the hole with one leg either side.

'Please let the jaws not miss me . . .'

*The monster was striding rapidly towards him*

The monster was now only yards from him.

Even Snatcher was caught up in the frenzy and was screaming commands. 'We have to get the cheese before those others get it! Open the jaws, drop the head, and CHOMP!'

Arthur watched as the monster lunged for him.

'Time for the hole!'

He breathed out, brought his legs together and put his arms straight up in the air. Arthur felt the cheese loosen around him as he dropped, then the bottom of the cheese hit the ground around the edge of the hole. There was a jerk as he fell free and continued down.

The jaws snapped down on the cheese. In the approaching mob, the cheese-lust turned to rage. 'It's got our cheese!'

'Get it before it swallows!'

The cheese-crazed mob fell upon the monster and started to tear it apart. Driven wild with desire they were fearless.

Snatcher and his crew knew that the fight was on. It was every man for himself.

Arthur's friends watched the mayhem with anxiety, uncertain exactly what was happening.

'Let us pray he managed to drop into the hole. I should never have allowed this,' Willbury said in horror.

The others kept quiet and most of them had their fingers crossed behind their backs.

It looked as if Arthur would be very lucky to survive. The mob were crawling over the monster like ants. Bits of the huge creature were torn away in the struggle. Then the 'cheese' appeared, held above the heads of the mob and the fighting grew more intense as figures jumped from the carcass of the wrecked monster to try to get to the cheese.

*The mob were crawling over the monster like ants*

'I can't bear to watch,' Willbury muttered as he turned away. The others strained their eyes in the hope of getting a glimpse of an un-injured Arthur.

It was becoming a vicious battle and in the melee the cheese hit the ground and shattered into a thousand pieces. The mob screamed and fell upon the fragments, kicking and fighting for every crumb.

'They look like a herd of starved pigs,' said a very worried Tom.

'Let's just hope they only eat the cheese,' replied Kipper.

As they watched the mob seemed to slow as it searched for the last tiny fragments. Then an eerie calm settled on the whole scene.

'We'd better go and rescue Arthur,' cried Kipper. This triggered a rush from the ship as Arthur's friends headed towards the hole, where they hoped he was still hidden.

As they got closer they had to push past the cheese maniacs to get to the hole.

Fish reached it first and looked down into the darkness. All he could see was mud and earth. Then the mud moved and a head emerged and blinked.

'Hello, Fish!'

*'I missed you so much!'*

Chapter 44

# THE WIND-UP . . .

The friends all let out their breath with relief that Arthur was all right. Then smiles crossed their faces.

'Thank heavens!' intoned Willbury.

Kipper joined Fish in pulling Arthur from the hole and what emerged was a very muddy and worried looking hero. Arthur looked about frantically. He saw what he was looking for near the edge of the now quiet mob.

'Grandfather!'

His grandfather looked rather blankly back at him. 'Arthur?'

Arthur ran to him and hugged him. 'I missed you so much. How do you feel? Are you all right?'

Grandfather thought for a moment. 'I'm not sure. Where am I?'

All around them the once crazed mob were sitting around looking bewildered.

Marjorie watched and then spoke. 'I think the antidote has taken effect. But it has left them a bit bamboozled.'

The mania was gone.

Then Bert sprang to life. 'We have to round up Snatcher and his mob. Let's be quick before they get their wits back.'

The pirates and rats quickly gathered up Snatcher and his men from amid the monster's wreckage and the confused huddles of now-cured cheese fiends, and tied them up.

Willbury watched as Snatcher was secured by Kipper and Tom.

*Snatcher was secured by Kipper and Tom*

'Look in his pockets. He might have those contracts we signed.'

Snatcher was in no state to protest, and Kipper searched him.

'Is this what you want?' he said pulling out a large wad of papers.

Willbury took them and flicked through them. 'Yes. I think it's getting cold. Shall we light a fire?'

Just as the ashes of the papers were being rubbed into the grass the Squeakers arrived.

'Right then. What's going on here?'

'These are the men that are behind the awful cheese mania that has been plaguing the town,' Willbury replied. Then he turned to where the doctor was standing amongst the crowd, not as yet tied up. 'And this "doctor" will explain everything. You might also like to contact the Edinburgh police and enquire about unsolved hair shaving crimes. I think you'll find he was very involved.'

The police had not had much luck recently and as they were paid by the number of arrests they made, they were very happy to have Snatcher, all his crew, and the doctor.

As the prisoners were led away to be locked up they began to recover and as they did it dawned on them how bad a predicament they were in. They were not happy and even though he was at the heart of it Snatcher took every opportunity when the police had not got their eyes on him to kick any of his men that got within reach.

'I don't think with all the trouble they've caused the town that they are going to escape justice this time,' Willbury observed to Marjorie. They both smiled.

Meanwhile the still recovering cheese maniacs wandered back home somewhat dazed and confused. This just left

Arthur and all his friends amongst the broken wreckage of the monster.

'I think we've all done rather well. Would anybody like to come back to the shop for a celebratory bucket of cocoa?' Willbury offered. 'I at least could do with a sit down.'

Arthur took his grandfather's hand and led him home. As they walked Grandfather slowly regained his old self, but fortunately not his old ills. Arthur told him of their adventures.

'Seems to me that you can take care of yourself,' said Grandfather.

Willbury, who had been quietly walking alongside, looked rather bashful and spoke. 'It's not just himself he can look after. I don't think any of us would have managed without him.'

'Thank you,' Arthur smiled. 'I did say I could be useful!'

*'I did I say I could be useful!'*

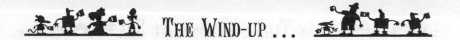 

Willbury just smiled back.

The shop became so full with Arthur and all his friends, that some had to sit on the stairs.

Upstairs in Arthur's bedroom sat a small group. The other boxtrolls and Titus were welcoming back their old friend Fish. Long into the night they asked him questions about the voyage and as he told them they shook their heads in wonder.

*Long into the night they asked him questions about the voyage*

Below them in the shop the party got a little wild. Bucket after bucket of cocoa was passed around, until they could take no more, but still everybody talked about their adventures.

Arthur sat by the fire close to Grandfather and they listened to the others.

'I wish I could have been there with you. I would have loved to have seen that island and the southern seas.'

Arthur smiled. He felt lucky, despite all the troubles they had.

'Next time!'

'I hope that is not going to be for a few weeks,' said Willbury. 'Unlike you, I need to recover.'

Willbury then stood and held up one of the almost empty buckets of cocoa.

'To Arthur. The finest, most courageous cheese there ever was.'

'ARTHUR!' shouted his friends.

*'Next time!'*

# THE HISTORY OF THE
# RATBRIDGE NAUTICAL LAUNDRY

For a number of years before the Laundry arrived in Ratbridge, it had operated as a pirate ship around the English and European coasts. It was not a terribly profitable enterprise, but it did survive. The crew were not a brave bunch and fighting was not really their thing. They liked the idea of being pirates and rather enjoyed dressing up and sailing, but going up against those who would not willingly part with their possessions seemed very disagreeable. It meant a lot of trouble and people getting hurt. No, they preferred trading in second-hand goods. These they would get from jumble sales in village halls in the various ports that they visited. As sailors most of them had learnt to sew and mend and this meant they were well equipped to recondition things.

For a long time this raised an adequate income to live on, but jumble sales slowly became less frequent, and a new trend started for cart sales. These were sales where people would load up their carts with anything they wanted to get rid of, and assemble in a field. Other people would then come to the field and buy whatever they fancied. This was harder for the pirates as the sales were usually held out of town and the pirates didn't have transport to get about on land. Tension grew over the months and tempers frayed as the budget got tighter. This finally came to a head with the food...

The ship's cook was a little brighter than most of those on board and spent most of his energy trying to make extra money by embezzling the food fund. He did this by substituting ingredients in his preparation of the rations. His name was Pungent. Pungent had a great imagination and he used this to create dishes that might (if good ingredients had been used) have been quite nice. But by cutting every corner in the making of them he produced only the vilest of dishes. In fish pie he would substitute seaweed for fish. This he would cook until it no longer had any colour and was so mushy that it could not be distinguished from fish that had also been boiled for as long. Instead of making a white sauce with butter, flour and milk, he would boil sawdust until it produced thin milky glue. Then instead of a cheese and potato topping he would boil socks down to make a flavouring that he added to recycled newspaper. The finished pie looked quite like a fish pie. It even had a vaguely cheesy smell, but it was certainly not fish pie and it tasted disgusting.

One of the things that sailors tended to live on was ship's biscuits. Most sailors had grown up with them and it was to these that the pirates turned when they found everything else inedible. Ship's biscuits were cheap to produce but Pungent could not bear to let another opportunity for profit go by. The ingredients should be flour and salt. These were made into stiff dough, rolled out flat, baked, and then left to dry out until very, very hard. But even with so cheap a recipe Pungent went to town. Over the months he reduced the amount of flour he used, replacing it with anything he could.

Finally he went too far.

Things had been bad on the jumble sale front for several weeks, and the crew were restless. Pungent was wandering the docks when he came across the remains of a piano. He had found that sawdust often worked very well as a replacement for flour in the biscuits—and here was something largely made of wood. Getting it on to the ship was no problem, breaking it up in grindable bits was no problem, but it was covered in black lacquer. He decided that he would tell the pirates that he had used whole grain flour. That ought to satisfy them if they asked questions. He put the wood through the mincer, then decided to bulk it up by throwing in all the ivory keys. The mincer produced a large pile of 'flour'. It had the faint odour of burning hair. Pungent added some seawater to the mix. After ten minutes of stirring he had produced a large grey ball. He squashed it out on the floor with his bare feet, and then cut it up into slabs. After putting them in the stove he turned up the heat and went to sleep in his hammock.

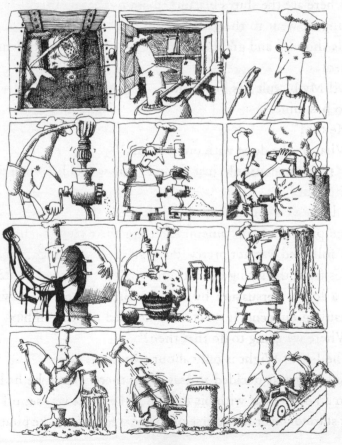

As lunchtime approached he took the biscuits out of the stove, retching at the appalling smell. He looked at them with pride—all grey and oily, with what looked like little teeth glinting in them. For the pirates' lunch, he knocked together a mixed grill from pieces of rubber boot and fried string. He placed the 'food' on a large salver and put it on the dining table in the main cabin. As usual the pirates reluctantly wandered in and sat down. Each took a few pieces of the fry-up and tried to eat. Each in turn gave up. Then came the usual cry.

'Where are the ship's biscuits? I am not eating this!'

Pungent went to the galley and brought out the new biscuits. Hands shot out and grabbed the biscuits. Then all was silent for a moment.

'Oi! My biscuit has bitten me!'

'So has mine!'

'Me too!'

'What has he done with our biscuits?'

'It's ornamentation! I just thought you would like something a bit different.'

'I'll give you something a bit different!'

The pirates lost no time in avenging their truly awful supper. What followed was not pretty. Pungent received a large number of bruises from the flying biscuits and was then dragged on deck. It took a lot of persuasion by the captain to stop the crew from keelhauling Pungent. It was finally decided to maroon him.

'Where we going to do that then?'

'The Isle of Wight is only about two hours away.'

And so it was decided to leave him there. When he had been put in an open boat with his own mixed grill he was set off and a party started. Over the course of the next few hours the pirates got very drunk and rather loud. Unlike many ships of its day, the *May Lou* had an engine and into its boiler the biscuits were thrown.

The party went on and as the biscuits burned the ship made good speed, unnoticed by the crew, on a path of its own choosing. The crew finally fell asleep and still the ship steamed on. Then it stopped.

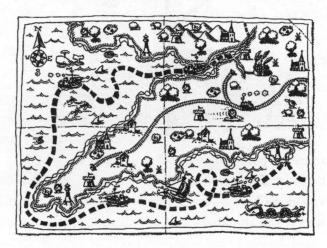

The next morning a mast flying a skull and crossbones was seen rising from behind the Ratbridge Gristle works. Word spread about the town like wildfire and soon more than half the town set off to find out more. A crowd had assembled on the canal bridge and along the towpath. For there—stuck under the bridge—was the front of a large ship.

Before long the hubbub of the crowd woke the crew from their slumbers. Groggy from their deep sleep, it took them some time to understand what had happened to their ship.

Optimistic at first, the crew set to and tried to free the ship, but to no avail. The crew then assembled on deck and a meeting was held.

'Well, it seems that we are stuck and broke!' said the captain.

'What are we going to do then?'

'Well, it's a Tuesday, and there won't be any jumbles till Saturday, and we have to eat. I suggest that we put our thinking hats on and try to think of some way to get ourselves out of this mess.'

'Well, let's look at what we know we can do?'

'We can plunder!'

'No, we can't! We are rubbish at that!'

'We could offer boat trips!'

'We're stuck, stupid! Boat trips mean moving!'

'We could open a laundry!'

All fell silent again

'Yes,' said the captain. 'We could open a laundry!'